It was him! Xander Tsakis.

The insignia on his helicopter was unmistakable.

Would everything change now?

An involuntary shiver gripped Rosy as the powerful aircraft cast a shadow over the playground. Would Xander Tsakis be any better for the island than his brother, Achilles? A great wave of concern for the children at the school washed over her. There was only one way to find out. She would go and see him, and ask what he meant to do to help them.

The next few minutes almost made Rosy change her mind.

Almost.

The helicopter swooped away and started flying low over the ocean. A door opened and a figure emerged. He was even more imposing than she had imagined. Barely clothed, his body was magnificent. Hard-muscled and tanned, there was no office pallor in sight. This billionaire looked exactly as the press described him: a ruthless, hard-nosed, polo-playing playboy. Which made it imperative to confront him right away, before he left on another of his global trips.

Susan Stephens was a professional singer before meeting her husband on the Mediterranean island of Malta. In true Harlequin style, they met on Monday, became engaged on Friday and married three months later. Susan enjoys entertaining, travel and going to the theater. To relax, she reads, cooks and plays the piano, and when she's had enough of relaxing, she throws herself off mountains on skis or gallops through the countryside singing loudly.

Books by Susan Stephens

Harlequin Presents

Snowbound with His Forbidden Innocent

Passion in Paradise

A Scandalous Midnight in Madrid
A Bride Fit for a Prince?

Secret Heirs of Billionaires

The Secret Kept from the Greek

The Acostas!

One Scandalous Christmas Eve
The Playboy Prince of Scandal
Forbidden to Her Spanish Boss
Kidnapped for the Acosta Heir

Visit the Author Profile page
at Harlequin.com for more titles.

Susan Stephens

UNTOUCHED UNTIL THE GREEK'S RETURN

Recycling programs
for this product may
not exist in your area.

ISBN-13: 978-1-335-59333-7

Untouched Until the Greek's Return

Copyright © 2024 by Susan Stephens

For questions and comments about the quality of this book,
please contact us at CustomerService@Harlequin.com.

Harlequin Enterprises ULC
22 Adelaide St. West, 41st Floor
Toronto, Ontario M5H 4E3, Canada
www.Harlequin.com

Printed in U.S.A.

UNTOUCHED UNTIL
THE GREEK'S RETURN

CHAPTER ONE

THE CALM BEFORE a storm was something a Romani could sense, but why here...why now?

Xander Tsakis had encountered this feeling only once before, when his life had taken a huge turn for the better, after a remarkable couple called Eleni and Romanos Tsakis scooped him up from the gutter and brought him home to raise as their son. What more could he ask of life now? Thanks to the miracle of their love, he had everything most men strived for and never had the chance to attain.

What form the impending storm would take remained to be seen, Xander reflected, raking a hand through his unruly black hair as he settled back on the plush, well-padded seat in his state-of-the-art custom-built helicopter. The aircraft was carrying him to the closest he'd ever come to a family home—the tiny island of Praxos, set like a gem in the sea off the west coast of Greece.

He hadn't always travelled in such luxury as this. Stealing a lift on the back of a refuse truck had been the closest he'd come to transport as a child. His rise from the gutter had been meteoric, though not without tragedy. The recent loss of his adoptive father, billionaire philanthropist Romanos Tsakis, was the latest in a series of losses that had dogged him throughout his life. Some might say his early years had been unusually hard, but hard had been his norm as a child.

Raised in a brothel by a series of women had accustomed him to change, and to the impermanence of everything in life, especially love. His Romani mother was said to have been barely sixteen when she'd given birth to him. A lack of care had led to her death, leaving newborn Xander to be passed around the brothel like the latest novelty. By the time he was six he had determined to forge a better life for himself, a desire fuelled by hanging around five-star venues when he was kicked out of the brothel at night, to prevent the local police, who frequented the establishment, from asking awkward questions about his presence there. Watching the rich and famous pour out of their limousines in fragrant splendour had been all it took to convince a street urchin that this was the life he craved.

Impossible though his dream might have seemed, his luck had changed on the day Romanos Tsakis had spied him rifling through the bins for food at the back of the Michelin starred restaurant where Romanos and his wife Eleni had just been celebrating their wedding anniversary. Being accosted by a strange man was nothing new for six-year-old Xander. Even in rags and filth, he was a good-looking child, but he was unusually savvy for one so young, which was how he had stayed safe on the streets. If the gypsy blood running through his veins had not insisted that this was the chance he had been waiting for, he might have settled for a cold meal of scraps.

Thankfully, time had proved his instinct about Eleni and Romanos correct, though his life before they had become a part of it had scarred him to the point where he could not give his trust easily, if at all. Romanos and Eleni were exceptions to that rule, but it had taken time for their love to break through Xander's self-inflicted barriers, and they'd only succeeded because they'd never given up on him. They were so full of love that, in time, he'd come to believe they were only short of halos.

It was just a shame their natural son, Achilles, had fitted the role of devil so well. Bigger and older by three years, Achilles had resented Xander from the off, and had done everything possible to drive him away. Only the promise of the education Xander had longed for, wedded to Eleni and Romanos's unfailing patience and love, made sure Xander stayed exactly where he was.

The flight he was taking today was to save an island ravaged by Achilles, following Eleni and Romanos's untimely deaths. He would stay at the Big House, as the Tsakis family home was known, where he had learned as a child that even the lives of good people could have a dark side. Achilles was that darkness. Today, there'd be no Eleni or Romanos waiting to greet him with the warmest of hugs. Eleni had died recently, and quite suddenly, sparing her the agony of the autopsy on Romanos and Achilles, that had found Achilles to be drunk at the wheel of his car when it went over a cliff with his father beside him.

When the tragedy happened he'd been working on a clean water project somewhere so remote he had no signal. By the time he was back in range the funerals of his father and brother had already taken place. Not being there had sent him half mad with grief, but he hadn't known the half of it, because his staff had thought it better not to tell him until he came home that Achilles had bled the island dry.

He should have been here to prevent the tragedy.

But he couldn't be in two places at once, and the clean water project had meant so much to Romanos.

Guilt still had its hold on Xander, and he moved restlessly as the familiar pain cut deep. 'Hover over the school,' he instructed the pilot to distract himself from a tragedy he couldn't change.

Education had been Romanos's driving imperative, and now it was his. Xander had experienced first-hand how education could encourage a guttersnipe like himself to dream big, and to achieve even more. Achilles had done so much damage in so short a time if the school was as rundown as the rest of the island he dreaded what he might find.

Curbing his anger, he put it in the same locked box containing all human emotion. Now Eleni and Romanos were gone, he had no reason to believe that he would ever meet their like again. But he could continue Romanos's good works. Reading Romanos's last message caused Xander's grip to tighten like a vice on his cell phone. His gaze lingered on the text, as if it might contain some small scrap of Romanos's goodness.

I've found a wonderful teacher for the school. A young woman named Rosy Boom. Look after her, Xander. Praxos can't afford to lose this one.

Guilt threatened to engulf him again. After Eleni's death, he had wanted to stay to support the grief-stricken Romanos, but the older man had begged him to see through to completion the clean water project that was the culmination of Romanos's life's work.

'You can do no good here,' he had insisted, *'but those people need you.'* And when he'd added, *'Their children deserve the same chance I gave you...'* Xander knew he had no option but to obey Romanos's request.

Sometimes, Xander believed Romanos was the only person who had ever truly understood him. For Romanos to leave this last message about a new teacher made it seem as if Romanos had suspected he wouldn't be around to steer the young woman through the difficult first few months of her life on the island. She spoke Greek, Xander had been told, having read Classics at university, before adding a teaching diploma to her quiver of achievements. He name-checked her again. Rosy Boom? Sounded more like an explosion in a flower store than a teacher. Had he already met her? Had she been on the island for Eleni's funeral? He searched his memory of that terrible day in vain, and was forced to concede that he'd been solely focused on supporting Romanos to the point where nothing else registered.

Banishing the young woman from his mind, he focused on his plan, which was to assess the problems created by Achilles before making things better than ever for the islanders who had suffered, however briefly, beneath the heel of a bully. Care of an island and its people might even answer the question of why, at the age of thirty-two, he hadn't married, and keep the press off his back for a while. The answer to that was simple. He'd never found a woman dynamic enough to interest him long-term, let alone one he'd trust with his heart. Better to focus his attention on his businesses and charities, which took him away so often he couldn't commit the time a wife would surely demand.

Shrugging off his jacket, he loosened his tie. Exhaling with relief, he released a couple of buttons at the neck of his shirt. Removing priceless diamond links, sparkling blackly on his crisp white cuffs, he tossed them onto the table in front of him.

Stretching his powerful limbs reminded him that he was a very physical man who just happened to have the knack of making vast sums of money. Reputed to be one of the foremost wealth creators on the planet, he was driven by his pledge to Romanos—to go out into the world with the sword of knowledge in one hand and the shield of Romanos's faith in him in the other. That was why he was so impatient to start work on returning Praxos to its former stability and happiness, after which he would move on, to plug yet another gap in the endless fight against hardship and poverty.

'We're almost over the school,' the pilot announced.

Xander ground his jaw in anticipation of seeing yet more dilapidation. Would the school even be open, without the funds Xander's staff had told him Achilles had stolen?

His surprised first impression was that everything was immaculate. Children were darting about the playground, playing tag with a young woman whom he guessed was the new teacher. When she saw his helicopter hovering overhead she stopped running and drew the children around her, as if to protect them.

'Thank you. Move on,' he instructed the pilot.

So, that was Rosy Boom. His sixth sense registered a connection of significance between them, but what that could possibly be, apart from her usefulness to him as a teacher recommended by Romanos, would remain a mystery for now.

Her skills as a teacher had to be the answer. Education was everything. From a distance, she wasn't particularly impressive. Scarcely taller than the tallest of her charges, apart from a wealth of auburn hair, strands of which had escaped the severe style into which she'd drawn it, she was hardly a beauty. But her first instinct had been to protect her students, which was a definite plus in her favour. She had no need to worry about the future of the school. Xander might be ruthless in business, but education was his lodestone, as it had been Romanos's, and he'd do nothing to stand in its way.

'Take us down to ten feet,' he instructed the pilot as the helicopter banked away to continue its journey along the coast.

Stripping off, he opened the cabin door. Naked, save for a pair of black silk boxers, he performed a perfect dive into the cooling embrace of the sea. There were treacherous currents beneath the surface, exactly like life, but he knew these waters well, since Romanos had brought him to live here at the age of six. The two months since his last visit had wrought many tragic changes, but the sea was the one constant, and it was here that he felt truly free. Making a silent pledge to the man who had raised him, he vowed to care for the island as Romanos had done, ensuring that Praxos and its people prospered.

It was him! Xander Tsakis. The insignia on his helicopter was unmistakable.

Would everything change now?

An involuntary shiver gripped Rosy as the powerful aircraft cast a shadow over the playground. Would Xander Tsakis be any better for the island than his brother Achilles? A great wave of concern for the children at the school washed over her. There was only one way to find out. She would go and see him, and ask what he meant to do to help them.

The next few minutes almost made Rosy change her mind.

Almost.

The helicopter swooped away and started flying low over the ocean. A door opened and a figure emerged. He was even more imposing than she had imagined. Barely clothed, his body was magnificent. Hard-muscled and tanned, there was no office pallor in sight. This billionaire looked exactly as the press described him: a ruthless, hard-nosed, polo-playing playboy. Which made it imperative to confront him right away, before he left on another of his global trips.

Balanced casually on the skids of the helicopter, he chose his moment, then executed a perfect swallow dive into the sea. Considering her inexperience where men were concerned, Rosy's body reacted with extraordinary enthusiasm to its first sight of an almost naked Xander Tsakis. Well, it could yearn all it liked, but this was Achilles' brother. They might not share the same blood, but could he be so different, having grown up alongside a fiend like that?

Shepherding the children back into school, Rosy firmed her jaw. Whoever, and whatever, Xander Tsakis turned out to be on closer inspection, she would confront him with her concerns about the school.

First things first: she had to get it through her head that Achilles was gone, and was never coming back, though each time she walked into the classroom it was as if the shadow of his leering face was lurking just around the corner. That day when he'd caught her alone and she'd felt the full, nauseating force of his rarely cleaned teeth invading her nostrils as he pressed her down on the desk... She shuddered now at the thought of it. If her friend and fellow teacher Alexa hadn't chosen that moment to come into the schoolroom, causing Achilles to lurch back with that sickly 'whatever's happened here, it's not my fault' sneer on his face, who knew what might have happened? Rosy was strong for her size, but Achilles had been stronger.

These children, and all the children who came after them, depended on their teachers to protect them and their school. Confronting Xander Tsakis couldn't wait. Hadn't the islanders suffered enough? Hardship under Achilles had been brief but devastating for everyone on Praxos. The Tsakis family owned the island and paid all the wages, until Achilles had started siphoning off the money for himself. Hardship had led to a barter system that was still working well, but it couldn't go on for ever. The islanders were already voting with their feet, leaving for the mainland in droves. If Rosy waited any longer to petition the last remaining Tsakis on the island there'd be no one left.

Bringing the children back to the forefront of her mind, she returned to the schoolroom, where they were preparing for Panigiri. This was a fiesta-type celebration which, in better times, when Eleni and Romanos had been alive, had involved the entire island. No money meant that it would have to be low-key this year. Everything depended on what the volunteers could give, lend or make. If Rosy had anything to do with it, the children would still play a full part and enjoy themselves. Panigiri symbolised the island's fight-back, and she was determined they would win.

The children's chatter soothed her, as they worked together on colourful bunting. Sitting cross-legged in a circle on the floor, it was hard not to get up now and then to glance out of the window in the vain hope of seeing Xander Tsakis again. Would he be clothed this time?

She kept those thoughts to herself and recalled the first time she'd met Romanos Tsakis, the man who had encouraged her to come and live here. He'd endowed a number of universities across the world, and had been the guest of honour at Rosy's graduation in London, where she'd spent an extra year earning her teaching qualification after graduating top of her year in her Classics degree.

From the very first time they'd met, she felt she could trust the elderly man. Rosy had been so immersed in learning about Greek culture, she'd even taken the time to learn the modern Greek language and he'd been thrilled when she'd spoken to him in his own language. As soon as Romanos had learned she spoke Greek he'd offered her a job on the spot, giving Rosy the perfect excuse to escape her own private torment.

She had never regretted her decision to come to Praxos. Nor would she now. Whatever type of man Xander Tsakis turned out to be, she would lay out the island's problems, and request his immediate attention to them. No way was she turning her back—

'Miss… Miss…' The children distracted her. Smiling, she praised their use of the English language, which was quickly becoming their second tongue, and one they loved to use with Rosy's encouragement. *'Eínai arketó kairó tóra?'* her charges chorused, eagerly displaying the bunting they'd made.

'Is this long enough now?' she translated slowly, inviting them to copy her as she spoke their words in English. 'Yes, it is,' she said, smiling as she repeated the phrase in Greek. *'Nai eínai.'* This year's Panigiri would be a celebration the island would never forget.

Would Xander Tsakis attend the celebration, or would he have left again by then?

He must attend. This year's Panigiri was crucial to the island's self-belief. And the islanders needed more than Xander's token presence. They needed his financial support. How else could the island recover?

Unwelcome awareness shivered down her spine as his hard, toned body flashed into her mind. She had to hope he'd show more respect than Achilles. He could hardly show less. She'd barely had chance to realise that she wasn't alone in the classroom when, with a guttural sound, Achilles had pounced, giving her no chance to escape, or to defend herself. Crossing her hands over her chest, she lightly traced the place on her arms where Achilles had bruised them.

Forget Achilles! Put him out of your mind!

Praxos was her home now, and she would fiercely defend what little Achilles had left them with. Rosy had no life to go back to in England. Before she came to the island her father's new wife had made it clear that Rosy was no longer welcome in her childhood home. Rosy would never deny her father a second chance at love after her mother's tragic death, but she worried that her stepmother's real interest was in her father's fast-dwindling funds, and the lovely home he and her mother had built together over many years.

'You deserve your own life,' Romanos had told her, when he'd offered Rosy the chance to teach on Praxos. Why had she confided in a man who was practically a stranger? Because her instincts had said Romanos was a good man. Who knew what made a person take one path over another? When her father begged Rosy to give him space to make his new relationship work, she knew those words were coming from a kind, gentle man, and had wanted nothing more than for her father to find happiness in his later years. His new partner's urging had taken on a rather more practical note, with Rosy finding her belongings, shoved roughly into a suitcase, waiting for her on the doorstep of a house that her key no longer fitted.

Putting that out of her mind, she concentrated on the work to be done now the school day had ended. Donning paint-streaked overalls, she continued redecorating the school. Later, she would beard the lion in his den, but there was enough time to repaint the picket fence, so when the children came to school the next morning everything would be dry to the touch, and they would have a bright and cheerful welcome.

Work day finally over, she returned inside to clean up. And jumped back in shock as the door she'd just closed swung open. Telling herself that Achilles was dead and would never again sneak about, waiting to surprise her, she was in no way reassured by the sight of the man standing in the doorway.

Xander Tsakis—at least he was clothed this time, though not in a city suit, or black boxer shorts, thank goodness, but in snug-fitting, well-worn jeans, a black top and serviceable boots. His hair was still wet, so he'd clearly come here straight from his dip in the sea.

'Ms Boom?'

His voice was brisk and deep, with barely the hint of an accent. And he did not look pleased. Now she saw why. His hand was covered in fence paint!

'My apologies, Kyrie Tsakis—I wasn't expecting you or anyone else, or I would have—'

'Would have what?' he interrupted. 'Put out a sign to say the paint was wet?'

'But I did—'

'Do you have something I can clean this off with?'

She flinched as he thrust a large, paint-streaked fist in her direction, and was again reminded that this was not Achilles. This was the man she'd barely glimpsed at Eleni's funeral, before he'd left for parts unknown.

'Of course,' she said, finding it difficult to concentrate while those extraordinary black eyes were staring searingly into hers. 'And by the way,' she added as she retrieved a bottle of white spirit and a clean cloth, 'welcome home—'

'To what?' he growled. 'Chaos?'

For someone who prided herself on her organisational skill that stung, but she let it pass because he was her boss, after all.

'I did put up a sign. It must have fallen over.'

'Clearly.'

Xander Tsakis towered over her like some otherworldly colossus, so shockingly good-looking she could hardly breathe. And though Achilles might have taught her to be wary, her body reacted with an alarming level of approval.

'At least you tried to close the gate,' she said as he began to clean the paint off his hands. 'And I appreciate your dropping by—'

'Am I being dismissed so soon?' This was said in a husky tone that made her heart pick up pace.

'No, of course not. As I just said, welcome, Kyrie Tsakis. Everyone on Praxos is thrilled you're back. The island needs you… The school needs you…' *I need you.* She actually gasped in absolute horror at almost saying that out loud.

The lift of one sweeping ebony brow suggested that not only had Xander read her thoughts, but he had dismissed her appeal out of hand.

'It's been a long day. You must be tired,' she blustered.

Xander gazed around, clearly interested in the colourful paintings Rose's pupils had completed in preparation for Panigiri.

'They've been working hard to create something special for the celebration,' she explained, glad to concentrate on something other than this most astonishingly masculine man.

A man more different from Achilles would be hard to imagine. Where Achilles had been plump and pasty-faced, with smooth red cheeks and bad breath, his adoptive brother was a model of rugged fitness, of bronzed perfection, of strong white teeth and a stern, towering omnipotence, who filled every inch of the simple classroom with his blistering charisma alone. And yet she felt no fear when she looked at him. Instead, she felt the light of battle fill her. It was time to take her chance—to stand up, stand firm and speak her piece.

'We're all expecting you to be here to cheer them on.'

No answer.

And then, 'Having seen the state of the rest of the island, I was keen to discover what was going on here.'

'I hope you're not disappointed?'

'Too early to tell.'

Fair enough, she supposed.

Xander Tsakis was such a force of nature he made Rosy uncomfortable in her own skin. She knew the type he favoured from the press coverage—though why she should be thinking about that, she had no idea, other than to say that none of those women had red hair and freckles, let alone thrift shop spectacles held together with tape.

'Right,' he said, turning as if he'd seen enough.

No. No! They still had to talk.

'Could you hang on a few moments to chat about the school?'

Slowly swivelling around to face her, he settled his sunglasses onto his nose. 'No,' he said bluntly, levelling a disturbing black stare into her eyes. 'I've a lot more to see, as I'm sure you can imagine.'

'Will you have the chance to talk tonight?'

'You're persistent.'

'I'll come to the house. What time would you like me to call?'

With a shake of his head, Xander lowered his brow to give her a look, but she wouldn't back down now, there was too much at stake.

'A thriving school is crucial to the recovery of the island.'

He continued to stare at her until she felt her cheeks burn red, but then she got the answer she'd hoped for. 'Eight o'clock sharp at the Big House.'

She did a quick calculation in her head and realised that her friend Maria, the Tsakis housekeeper, would still be on duty, so Rosy wouldn't be alone there with him. 'Eight o'clock sharp,' she repeated.

Xander hummed as he reached for the door handle, adding only, 'Don't be late.'

Resisting the urge to salute, she followed him to close the door.

'Who are these people in the pictures?' he asked suddenly.

Xander had stopped so abruptly she almost bumped into him.

'Your parents,' she explained, backing away a few

steps. The power he exuded completely eclipsed that of Achilles, and she wasn't ready to trust another man yet, especially another member of that family. 'The children insisted your parents must be part of our celebrations, and so they painted their portraits.'

'Eleni and Romanos would be touched,' Xander admitted with an expression on his face that gave her a hint that this was no mindless oaf like Achilles, but a thoughtful, sensitive man of a different type completely. 'I can never forget their kindness to me.'

Nor could Rosy, which was why she had never told them that their son Achilles had attacked her when she'd turned him down.

'I'm very sorry. This return to the island must be so hard for you.'

He swung around and the force of his stare ripped right through her. 'Life moves on, and we must move with it.'

Did Xander really think it was so easy to deal with loss? Maybe he didn't feel much of anything? But she knew that was wrong, for in those few moments when he'd looked at the children's pictures she had seen something in his eyes, and it was a grief that matched her own.

'How do you afford the raw materials for this work? I was told that there were no funds available for anything at all.'

'That is true, but we have instigated a barter system, and it's working really well. I tutor the local decorator's children, for example, and he gives me paint for the school.'

'How very enterprising.'

Was he being sarcastic?

'Necessity makes survivors of us all.'

'Here endeth today's lesson?' Xander suggested dryly.

Rosy could have bitten off her tongue. Xander's ex-traordinarily difficult childhood had been well documented in the press. How could she have forgotten how he'd suffered before Romanos had found him?

'Survival of the island is vital, for everyone's sake,' he agreed, to her relief, after testing her with another of his brooding black stares. 'But you should be doing more than survive here on Praxos. We will talk more about this tonight.'

And with that he turned and strode away.

'Watch the wet paint!' she called out in panic.

Xander's response was a raised hand. Returning inside, she collapsed onto one of the small, hard chairs. What had just happened? Xander Tsakis had taken control of the situation, Rosy concluded, wondering if it was possible to recover from their first meeting before eight o'clock tonight.

Elbows on knees, face in hand, she remained where she was for all of five seconds, before leaping to her feet in a panic. Flinging the door wide, she was in time to see Xander fold his powerful frame into an aggressive red muscle car. 'Don't stamp on the gas! Dust! Wet paint! Okay,' she muttered as he appeared not to hear. 'See you later…'

Bracing herself, she prepared for her work on the fence to be ruined, but Xander drove away as slowly as she could have wished—until he reached the end of the lane when, with a roar like a thunderclap, his low-slung vehicle screamed out of sight, powered by an unknowable dark force…who might turn out to be a force for good or for bad.

CHAPTER TWO

NARROWING HIS EYES, Xander stared into the rear-view mirror, the first glimmer of humour he'd felt in a long while curving his mouth. In spite of Romanos's strong recommendation, he'd had a few doubts about the new teacher. Cold facts suggested Rosy Boom was too young at twenty-four to hold such a responsible position. Having met the woman, he realised he should have trusted Romanos's judgement.

Not only was Kyria Boom clearly equal to the task, she had the mettle to stand up to him. There weren't many people who could say that. There was steel in those astonishingly beautiful emerald-green eyes. Even shielded by the cheapest spectacles he'd ever seen, they'd fired warning darts at him. What a refreshing change. Great wealth generally brought sycophants flocking, and he welcomed the challenge of a woman who knew her own mind. What he'd seen of her work with the children had impressed him, but it was the way she'd blushed when their hands had brushed that most intrigued him. She wasn't his type or even close to it, but for some reason—that sixth sense again, perhaps—he felt a distinct warning that this time, if he was serious about keeping his interest in a woman confined to mutual physical satisfaction, it was he who should be on his guard.

He wasn't too worried. He had a plan that would keep her too busy for either of them to fall into any kind of temptation, and he was keen to see how she coped with a suggestion that would stretch anyone to their limit.

Before he turned onto the main road he couldn't resist one more glance into the rear-view mirror. Rosy Boom was staring after him. No wave. No acknowledgement of any kind. What was in her mind? Would she be equal to his challenge? Surprising himself, he hoped that would be the case.

Back in the Big House, the mellow state that had come over him since his encounter with the teacher was abruptly cut short. Even the dim light of late afternoon couldn't mask the stains on the tapestry seat cover he remembered Eleni working on so diligently to brighten Romanos's study. Seeing evidence of Achilles' wrecking ball approach to everything precious first-hand made him rage inwardly.

When Eleni was alive Achilles had been forced to toe the line. Never had there been a better example of the steel hand within a velvet glove than Eleni Tsakis but, with Eleni gone, Xander in a far distant land and Romanos scarcely able to think straight for grief at the loss of his believed wife, none of the servants would have dared to challenge Achilles. They knew his spiteful temper and must have stayed well out of his way. And this was the result.

There were rings on the polished surface of a cherished antique desk, where he could picture Achilles banging down a hot mug of coffee as he called some whore, or the betting shop. This was the same desk where Romanos had dispensed so much good, not just for the island but the entire world.

Settling down in Romanos's big leather chair, he welcomed a distraction in the shape of the redoubtable Rosy Boom, who, in spite of his best efforts to eject her from his mind, had stayed resolutely put. Glancing at the clock on the wall, he realised he was actually impatient to see her again. But then guilt overcame him in this room where the very essence of his father still remained. All the surface damage could be repaired. What couldn't be changed was the fact that he'd been on the other side of the world when Romanos was killed. He'd missed his funeral and that was hard to bear.

How could so much change in a matter of two short months? Banishing that unhelpful thought from his mind, he did as Romanos would have wanted him to do and focused solely on the future.

Back in the quaint shoreside boarding house where Rosy was lucky enough to have the most beautiful attic room overlooking the seashore, she was stressing about her upcoming meeting with Xander Tsakis. Having only caught a brief glimpse of him at Eleni's funeral, it had been impossible to prepare for the shock of seeing a man with such blazing good looks up close. He was a complete contrast to her simple life on the island. Even in jeans, Xander Tsakis radiated style, sex and sophistication.

Thank goodness she had the chance to ground herself

here in her simple, airy room before seeing him again tonight. Initially paid for by Romanos, the room was a perk of Rosy's job, and when Achilles had stolen all the money that paid for it, the owners had simply gifted it to her for as long as she wanted to stay, in return for Rosy giving their children extra English lessons.

Pulling faces at herself in the mirror, she had to believe her homely looks would have no bearing on her meeting with Xander. Not everyone was preened and buffed to the nth degree, even though, if she scrolled through Xander's appearances in the press, it looked as if that was the only type of individual he came across. Thanks to the almost ever-present sunshine, her freckles were more pronounced than ever, and her hair had always had a mind of its own. Bad enough it was the colour of marmalade, without it being so wild and wavy. Scraping it back, she secured it in a severe coil at the nape of her neck. It was vital for the school that Xander Tsakis took her seriously.

Spectacles on. Straight face. But she couldn't keep that up for long. She only had to remember the children she taught, the fun they always had together and how responsive they were to learning for her face to soften in a smile. And when money allowed—if it ever did—she would treat herself to a new pair of glasses. Meanwhile, the tape she'd wrapped around the bridge of this old pair worked just fine, even if it did rub her nose.

Heart racing at the thought of leaving for the Big House, she knew it couldn't be put off any longer. Grabbing a rare barter treat, a straw hat she'd exchanged for a punnet of strawberries grown by herself in the guesthouse garden, she crammed it on and raced down the stairs, calling out a fond goodbye to her hosts.

They called back, thanking her for the chocolate brownies she'd baked to surprise them. It was the little things that made people happy, Rosy reflected as she headed at speed for a shortcut across the sand.

Xander towelled down roughly after his shower. Securing it around his waist, he strolled across his bedroom. Leaning against the side of the window, he stared out. He never tired of this view. Even when the sun began to dip in the sky the froth-fringed sea was a ravishing sight.

Pulling away from the wall, he checked the time. Would she be late? In his opinion, poor timekeeping demonstrated a lack of interest. Romanos had selected this woman for a very special task, but he'd hired her when things were running smoothly. Did she have what it took to restore and rebuild? He'd done his research on her and had deduced that Rosy gathered children around her to fill a gap left by the absence of family. Some might say he accumulated business deals to fill that same gap.

Easing his neck, he stretched his muscular frame. There was much to do, and no time to stand around thinking about it. Either she was up to the job he had in mind or he'd find a suitable replacement.

A last glance out of the window stopped him in his tracks. There was no mistaking the young woman jumping in and out of the surf as she hurried along the beach. Shoes in hand, she was splashing and kicking at the waves with abandonment. If he tried hard enough, he might remember what that felt like. He too had enjoyed the beach when he was growing up because, he realised now, Eleni and Romanos had given him the freedom to enjoy childhood for the first time in his life.

Yes. Do it, he urged her silently as the young school-teacher stopped and raised her hands to her hair. Plucking the hat from her head, she freed her glorious waves from the cruel style, as he'd hoped she would. Throwing her head back, she laughed as the breeze tossed the auburn abundance about in a cloud of fire to rival a burnished sunset. He imagined the sounds of pleasure she was making as she turned her face towards the sky. Too soon she was on the move again, keen not to be late, he guessed. She stopped once more to finger-comb her hair into some semblance of neatness. That done, she rammed the hat back on her head and started to skip in his direction. If she wanted him to think of her as serious-minded and diligent, Rosy Boom had just revealed another side of herself, and it was that side he found intriguing.

He stepped back as she suddenly gazed up at his window. She couldn't have seen him watching, so had she sensed his interest? Her manner changed, and she began to walk swiftly and with purpose towards the house. The set of her jaw was firm and her expression was one of sheer determination. That was the image he'd find hard to forget.

It might be an idea to get dressed before she arrived. Raking his hair into some sort of order, he turned to tug on his jeans.

Eight o'clock prompt.
She'd made it.

Rosy breathed a sigh of relief. Her smile widened when Xander's housekeeper opened the door. 'Maria!' They were already great friends, having met countless times before in the village.

'Come in, come in—I love your hat,' Maria exclaimed and the next thing Rosy knew, she was being enveloped in the warmest of hugs. 'You look lovely tonight,' Maria declared as she took charge of the precious hat and laid it carefully on the hall table.

'At least I'm not late,' Rosy replied with relief as she smoothed her hair.

'Ready to meet the great man?'

'We've already met, actually... But I am ready. For anything,' Rosy confirmed.

Maria's dark eyes twinkled. 'I'm sure you'll have the measure of him before you know it.'

Rosy hummed. But as they walked deeper into the house she began to doubt everything she was here for. How was she going to persuade a man like Xander Tsakis to invest both his time and his money in a struggling island? Might he prefer to cut his losses and move on? Yes, Praxos had belonged to the Tsakis family since time immemorial, but Xander was known to travel the globe endlessly, rarely stopping for long in one place. Replacing paint-stained dungarees with a modest navy dress was hardly going to swing her argument for her.

It occurred to her then that maybe he usually dressed for dinner. But there didn't appear to be any other guests. And she hadn't been invited for dinner, Rosy reminded herself as Maria drew to a halt outside an impressive mahogany door. So much depended on this meeting. Sucking in a deep steadying breath, Rosy lifted her chin in readiness to confront the future of the island in rampant male form.

'What more could I want than this?' she murmured, unaware that she had spoken out loud.

'For Xander to stay on the island?' Maria suggested.

'Do you think he will?' Her mouth felt dry as Maria knocked politely on the door.

'Perhaps you can persuade him to stay.'

Rosy huffed at that, but for the sake of the island she had to try.

'Come…'

That single word, delivered in a deep and very masculine husky tone, resonated through her like a long-lost chord. Now she was being ridiculous, Rosy told herself firmly as the door swung open. Gathering courage around her like a cloak, she gave Maria one last purposeful look and then walked into the room, but as Maria closed the door behind her, emotion hit her all at once. The last time she'd been here was with Romanos, not so long ago. She missed him so much, and realised now that she had thrown herself into work to cope with his loss. What made it worse was that Romanos had made this room a warm haven, yet now in his place stood a cold, impassive man.

'Kyrie Tsakis,' she said politely, lifting her chin to meet an assessing gaze that managed to be cold yet burned with a dangerous fire. 'Thank you for calling by the school earlier, and for making time to see me tonight.'

'Xander, please,' he insisted, but his tone did not encourage informality. 'Won't you sit, Kyria Boom?' He indicated a chair in front of his desk while it appeared that he would remain standing.

'Call me Rosy, please.' She chose to remain standing too, and so they ended up stubbornly confronting each other for a few potent moments.

'I'd prefer it if you sat.' He angled his chin towards the chair again.

This was not the time to be awkward. She was here to speak to him on behalf of everyone on the island.

'I see you've noticed the changes,' he remarked as her gaze lingered on the careless ring marks left on a beautiful desk.

She said nothing, but they both glanced to where a piece had been chipped out of the door, where someone must have slammed it in a temper. She could only hope that Xander would be more respectful of the things that had meant so much to his parents than Achilles had been. He'd placed his glass of water on a mat, she noticed, so maybe she could dare to hope.

'Would you like a drink?' he offered.

'Water would be great. Thank you.'

'So, what is it you've come here to say?' he asked, having placed a second drinks mat in front of her.

'I'd like to discuss my concerns for the school.'

'And your future at that school, I presume?'

'I'd be lying if I didn't say that I'm concerned about my future,' Rosy admitted, wondering if she'd ever encountered such a compelling stare before. 'But I'm much more worried about the children I teach. And their parents, of course. A barter system can only stretch so far, and the island is severely struggling.'

* * *

Everything about this woman appealed to him, from the straightforwardness of her words and her level stare, right down to her ample breasts, so full, so lush, and so tightly bound beneath a dress that did her no favours at all. Even the stubborn set of her jaw provoked him in a pleasurable way, igniting all his hunting instincts. He'd seen that streak of wildness in her on the shore, and it was that which drew him. She was not his usual choice when it came to women. No commitment, no long-standing arrangement, no unwanted emotion was his mantra, and a code his usual partners fully understood, but there was something different about this woman, something that told him she would not roll over for his pleasure in any sense. He liked that about her most of all.

Closing off all personal thoughts, he concentrated on the task at hand, which was to find people to help him understand the island's woes so he could solve them, restore order and contentment, and then move on to his next project.

'Rest assured, the education of the island's children was my father's priority, as it is mine. Without education, no one can progress. I trust that reassures you?'

'Time will tell,' she said, surprising him yet again with her directness.

He might have challenged those words, but for the concern and dedication in her eyes.

'The last time I was here was to see your father,' she explained. 'He is a great loss to the island.'

'He is indeed,' he agreed, looking away as she put a

hand over her heart, but the damage was already done. Her breasts were truly spectacular. 'Do you see yourself taking part in the rebuilding of the island?'

He turned back to face her in time to see hope leap in a gaze as frank as it was determined.

'Of course,' she exclaimed. 'I'll do anything.' And then, incredibly, she added, 'Will you?'

'What do you think, Kyria Boom?' he demanded.

'I don't know. I don't know you. And please call me Rosy.'

He could think of a lot of things to call her, and none of them were as delicate as that flower.

'It will take more than teams of workmen from the mainland to put things right on Praxos. So much damage has been done in so short a time, and not all of it is visible,' she said, illustrating her remark by trailing her fingertips across the damage on the desk. 'Your biggest task, as I see it, is to rebuild trust, and for that you'll need insiders who've lived through it.'

'Are you offering your services, Kyria Boom?'

Her emerald stare pinned him. 'Are you asking?' she challenged, as if they were on equal terms.

'Yes,' he admitted, 'I am.' He liked that she wasn't afraid to confront him, but it was time to set some rules. Planting his fists on the desk, he leaned towards her. 'Your job is to keep the school open—'

'I'll do anything to make sure of that,' she cut in. 'All I think about every day is—what would your father want me to do? I realise your grief over his loss is far greater than mine, so forgive me for mentioning his name, but just being here in Romanos's study...'

'Grief is grief,' he observed in a clipped tone.

Straightening up, he moved away from the desk. 'We must all deal with loss in our own way.'

'Or not at all,' she fired back.

When he turned, she met his warning stare with a level gaze. 'Time to move on,' he decreed with a closing gesture.

'Of course.' She frowned. 'Shall I come back when you're—'

'In a better mood?' he suggested.

'When you've had chance to rest,' she countered. 'You must have been travelling for some time today.'

'I'm used to it.'

'Forgive me if I've upset you. It's just the school means so much to me.'

'All I need to know right now is: will you stay?'

'Question or instruction?' she shot back as she got to her feet. 'Of course I'll stay. The school means everything to me.'

When her emerald eyes fired that message into his the urge to palm those breasts and kiss the defiance out of this woman, with her feisty mouth and make-do-and-mend spectacles, overwhelmed him, but he was all about control, and she was nothing like the women who usually hovered around him. There'd be no begging him to seduce her. She'd more likely pin him down with her sharp tongue and that emerald fire stare. So be it. He looked forward to it. He couldn't remember a time when his control had ever been tested like this, but flexing that muscle was a good thing.

'Sit down,' he rapped as she headed for the door, adding belatedly in a very different tone, 'please…'

She turned. She looked him straight in the eye. She

walked slowly back to the desk and took her seat again, while he stood across from her with the desk between them.

'I realise I could have made a better start,' she admitted, lifting her face to his, 'but passions are running high. This is our chance—your return, I mean. Praxos can only fully recover with your help.'

And with people like you willing to fight for it, he thought with reluctant admiration.

'I'll do anything you want me to,' she assured him.

But only for the school, he reminded himself, not in his bed.

He shrugged. 'I'm sure you will.'

She amused him, and it was a long time since anyone had achieved that. There had been a regrettably long line of women, not one of whom had raised a laugh from him.

'Why is the Panigiri so special to you?'

Her face lit up. 'It's a celebration of life,' she exclaimed, as if this were obvious. 'And after so much sadness on Praxos recently... Oh, sorry—I've done it again. I don't mean to keep on upsetting you.'

'You haven't. Go on.'

'The island needs a reason to celebrate more than ever—' She could barely contain her excitement. He would have to be totally insensate not to wonder how all that passion would translate to his bed. 'The islanders miss your parents, especially the children—'

'I get that everyone needs a chance to grieve,' he said with a let's-move-this-on gesture.

'Even you,' she said, bringing everything to a dead halt.

He resented her interference. 'Don't waste your time worrying about me.'

'No? Why not?'

Her expression was so full of concern he couldn't bring himself to fire back a cutting remark.

'Let's just stay on topic. Tell me more about the island's problems with money. Romanos had plenty of money. The extra I sent was to fund additional projects that Romanos might not have budgeted for.'

'Achilles didn't care where the money came from. His extravagance had to be funded.' She shrugged. 'And that was that.'

Guilt poleaxed him. Achilles had sworn he had changed, and had begged for a chance to prove himself by taking care of their father. If Achilles hadn't used Romanos as a bargaining tool, Xander might not have been persuaded to go, but to hear from Achilles that he had felt shut out as a child made the decision for him. Achilles had deserved his chance, and Xander's departure for the remote clean water project, so close to his father's heart, had felt like the right thing to do. *'Don't worry,'* Achilles had begged him. *'I've changed. Romanos has changed me. As he changed you...'* And those words had reminded Xander that when he'd first joined the Tsakis family he'd stolen food from the kitchen and kept a stash beneath his bed—just in case the manna from heaven stopped falling. He'd hidden every penny Romanos had ever given him, in another hiding place beneath the floorboards in his bedroom, *just in case* he had to run away.

'I can see I've upset you,' Rosy said, jolting him back to the present. 'I hope you stay long enough to enjoy the island. I find that sometimes nature can heal when all else fails—'

'Yes. Thank you,' he said, cutting her off, unwilling to face his feelings, especially in front of this woman.

'And I realise there's a lot of work ahead, but—'

'But *what*?' he interrupted sharply. Did she ever take a hint?

Instead of retaliating, she stood and faced him with compassion in her eyes. 'Just promise me one thing.'

'Promise you what?' he demanded incredulously, neither wanting nor needing her concern. But Kyria Boom continued undaunted.

'Don't just throw money at the problem. Stay here— get to know the island again. Everyone's missed you, so, if you can, make time to meet and mingle with the people. They'd really appreciate it, and they'll tell you what Praxos needs. And try to find time for yourself— walk on the beach, plan, think, dream—'

'I'll leave dreaming to you,' he assured her with a glance at the door.

It was a shock when her face crumpled. To see such a strong woman on the point of breaking down caught his attention more than any words could.

'Don't make the islanders suffer because of me,' she begged.

'I'm not sure I understand you. I have no intention of making anyone suffer. And you've done nothing wrong,' he felt bound to add. 'I'm sure we'll talk again—' He moved ahead of her to open the door.

Before you leave? her eyes asked him, as clearly as if she had spoken out loud.

Nothing was set in stone, and he would make no false promises.

'When will we speak again?' she asked as she stood in his way.

CHAPTER THREE

WHAT WAS SHE DOING, butting heads with this primal force of nature—who just happened to be her boss? He held her future, and that of the school, in his big, capable hands. Yes, she had every reason to care about Praxos, but Xander Tsakis had suffered far more. He hadn't just grown up in poverty, he'd survived starvation, neglect and who knew what else. And now he'd lost the people who'd saved him from that. Wouldn't anyone want to turn their back on all the reminders? If she wasn't careful, he might never visit Praxos again.

Gathering herself, she went in for one last appeal. 'Every ship needs a captain, and you're it,' she stated firmly.

'Are you instructing me?'

His expression was incredulous, and she didn't need anyone to tell her that no one had ever spoken to Xander Tsakis like that before.

'I'm just stating facts,' she said calmly.

Beautiful, heavily fringed eyes were as hard as black diamonds, and glittered with ferocious power. Would she blink in their beam or back down? Not a chance.

'I'll do anything I can to help you, and I'll stay for

as long as it takes. All I ask in return is that your commitment to this island never falters. After what they've been through, our mutual friends and neighbours need the type of certainty that only you can provide.'

Xander uttered a weary, almost theatrical sigh. 'Sit down again. Before you go, you'd better tell me more about yourself, so I can understand your passion for this island.'

Yes!

'Where would you like me to start?' And why, exactly, did she have to rip her gaze away from his stern mouth as she asked the question?

'Wherever you'd like to begin,' he drawled, and she was convinced he was staring at her mouth now.

Xander sat across from her as she told him a little about her life. Becoming more confident as she went along, she seemed to forget he was there, as if these memories had waited a long time to be released. He enjoyed watching her talk. He liked watching her lips move. It was only a small step from there to imagining so much more her lips could do.

But some things were more important, because they told him more about her—things like Rosy's wistful smile as she recounted her past. She'd been happy when her mother was alive, but when her father had married again everything had changed for the worse. His respect for her grew as she described her pathway to freedom. It was well thought out, well planned, and featured education in every detail. When Romanos had offered her the job teaching on Praxos, she'd seen an opportunity to build a new life for herself.

Rosy talked more about others than herself, and how various people had influenced her choices, but she also made it clear that she held the casting vote. Her main interest was in educating the children of the island. Her resentment when Achilles had all but closed the school was palpable, but she had approached this problem in the same way that she approached everything else, with calm reason, as she explained how she had helped the school survive. When she told him that getting to know each child was like digging for treasure, he was sold.

Where had this woman come from? How unerring was Romanos's aim when it came to choosing someone outside his family to better the lot of the people of Praxos? Romanos had been right to message him about Rosy, but her value to the island was plain to see.

'My father did well, appointing you,' he remarked when she'd finished.

'Does that mean I get to keep my job?'

If she'd been beautiful before, the radiance on her face now transcended everything. Even the beat up spectacles couldn't hide an inner beauty like Rosy's.

Romanos and Eleni had eventually taught him to love again, when the six-year-old child he'd once been had thought love was for other people—the people he'd seen in posh restaurants, who always looked so happy. But with Eleni and Romanos gone, it was as if their healing love had gone with them, allowing the pain of the past to return full force, giving him nightmares, sending him back to a time when he'd had to hide from perversion and hunt for food in the trash. Of course he'd researched the brothel since then. He had contacts, and police records had made that easy. The image of his mother, looking no more than a child herself, lying dead on a slab, would stay with him for ever.

Would everyone leave him? Was he a jinx? If that were true, he should stay well clear of Rosy.

'I've made so many plans for the children...' he realised Rosy was explaining. Her purity shattered the dark thoughts in his head, replacing them with light and hope, as she added, 'If you support me, we'll never have to let those children down.'

He held up a hand to silence her. 'There's no doubt you have a natural flair for teaching—and organising. Which gives me an idea...' One he'd been harbouring for all sorts of reasons, from the first moment they'd met.

Rosy's emerald eyes sparkled with eagerness behind their shield of glass.

'The Panigiri?' he prompted. 'You must only have a limited budget for that?'

'Barely anything,' she admitted sadly. 'We're relying on donations and hard work to make things happen.'

'So, to give the island the boost it needs, and to underline the fact that I intend to return everything to how it was in my father's time—if not better, I'm prepared to fund the Panigiri to the tune of—'

As he mentioned the sum he had in mind, she gasped out loud. 'We won't need that much.'

'I'll expect you to keep a tight budget. These things always cost more than you think. I'll put my team at your disposal, but you'll be in overall charge. Do you think you can do that?'

'Yes,' she said without hesitation.

'Good. Your success at the school, together with the

fact that you were behind the whole bartering system in the first place— Yes, I have done my research,' he assured her when she started to speak. 'This project will test you, but I don't believe you'll fail, if only because backing down doesn't seem to be in your nature. Plus, you have the passion, as well as intelligence, and you know the islanders. You've made your home here, and you've been accepted, so they trust you. I expect spreadsheets, and a full account of all the money you spend,' he said, standing up.

'It will take more than money,' Rosy exclaimed, standing too. 'It will take heart.'

He hummed with his usual cynicism. 'Let's just agree on your vision and my cash. Deal?' He held out his hand to shake hers.

'Deal,' she said, putting her tiny hand in his.

Why did she affect him so deeply? Because she made no attempt to flirt with him like all the others? Honest and direct, she seemed not to care about the power he wielded, or the wealth he possessed. They were just two people with one aim in mind, which was to bring stability back to Praxos. *One aim in mind?* His straining groin told another story entirely!

Clearing his throat, he said briskly, 'Excellent. How quickly can you get things moving?'

'Let me talk to my friends, liaise with your team, and I'll get back to you.'

Good answer. He doubted she'd ever done anything like this before, but she had no intention of being rushed.

Could she do this? She had to, Rosy determined. Hadn't she filled a place on the college council, when no one else was prepared to do that? Who was the mouse in the corner, drawing up a sturdy skeleton for the social committee to work from? Yes, she knew spreadsheets. She'd used them to organise that committee's unformed ideas into a workable scheme. Managing huge budgets had never been mentioned when Romanos first hired her, but things had changed drastically since then and for the sake of the school she must change with them.

'Our first meeting will be—'

'Next week?' she suggested, thinking that would give her plenty of time to form teams and liaise with Xander's people.

'Next week?' Xander's frown transformed his swarthy face into stern and commanding lines in a way that made her rebellious body yearn. 'I expect daily meetings, starting tomorrow at noon,' he said.

'Okay.' She'd make that work somehow. She must.

What now? The look in his eyes that made her senses stir was back again, and she was having enough trouble as it was hiding the fact that her heart was racing and she couldn't get enough air into her lungs. Being attracted to Xander wasn't remotely convenient, but there was nothing she could do about it. His particular brand of male potency was impossible to ignore, and her largely untried body was responding as if she were starving and facing a feast.

'Before I go—' she said, collecting herself rapidly.

'Yes?'

That single word, delivered in a deep, husky tone, stroked her senses until they were in danger of scrambling too. 'Before we meet again, I'd ask you to open a Panigiri-specific bank account, so I can keep every transaction regular from the start.'

Xander dipped his chin as he considered this. 'That seems sensible.'

Three short words that any employee might hope to hear in similar circumstances, but this was no ordinary boss. Xander Tsakis spoke with his eyes, and they conveyed a lot more than he was saying. There was a deep, searching interest... And an undeniable heat.

Surely not? Surely not heat?

But, as inexperienced as she was, there was no denying the electricity sparking between them. She'd never felt so alive, or so aware of anyone before, which made her doubly careful not to brush against him as he led her towards the door.

'Surprise me,' he said as they crossed the hall. 'Exceed my expectations.'

Rosy's heart lifted as she wondered if that meant he would stick around, at least long enough to enjoy the final result.

'Don't forget your hat—'

She glanced up as Xander angled his chin in the direction of her market stall straw.

'Good luck,' he added, as she crammed it on. 'I look forward to our meeting tomorrow.'

So did she. Just being in Xander's company was enough to excite and enthuse.

'By which time, you'll have details of the bank account you've opened for the Panigiri,' she said, speaking her thoughts out loud.

'When I need a reminder, Kyria Boom, I'll ask for one.'

Just like that, Xander stuck his spear into her little fantasy of Rosy and her drop-dead gorgeous boss sailing off into the Panigiri sunset together. Not for the first time, she was reminded that it didn't do to allow her inner passionate nature free rein, not even for one single careless moment.

'Until tomorrow,' she said brightly, and was rewarded with a grunt.

Back on the beach, she stared up at the lantern moon, certain that a man like Xander Tsakis would never waste his time on a woman with scraped back hair and thrift shop spectacles, but she could dream, couldn't she? When she'd first come to the island, Rosy had worn her hair down, or sometimes in a ponytail, with contact lenses to improve her sight, rather than this ancient pair of specs. She'd laughed and enjoyed life, outside the schoolroom as well as in, without realising that Eleni and Romanos's natural son, Achilles, had noticed more than her ability to teach school.

She'd been working late one evening when he'd called in. At first he'd been respectful, asking questions about the children's work, but then he'd trapped her against the desk, holding her in a bruising grip and thrusting her back roughly until she was lying half on top of it. If Alexa, the elderly headmistress, hadn't arrived at that precise moment there was no telling what might have happened. Thankfully, Achilles had plenty of female admirers on the mainland, and with Alexa keeping guard from then on he'd soon lost interest in the village schoolteacher.

There was nothing to suggest that Xander was the same as Achilles, but nothing to say he was different.

Only time would prove who he truly was, and even then she had to learn to trust her own instincts.

'If I have to leave the island for any reason—'

She almost jumped out of her skin, hearing his voice at her back.

'Sorry. I didn't mean to startle you. I just wanted to say that if I have to leave the island for any reason, Maria will be the first to know.'

And his housekeeper was supposed to tell everyone? Why couldn't Xander speak to the people who mattered? Brushing off her questions, along with her shock at seeing him so soon, she admitted, 'Sorry I jumped. I didn't expect you to follow me home.'

'I realised I didn't want to let you walk back in the dark on your own.'

Because she'd just been thinking about Achilles she felt a moment of apprehension. The night was dark. There was no one around. Suddenly, it was hard to breathe easily. She had to reason sensibly, that Xander was standing some distance away and, thanks to the brightness of the moon, she could see the concern for her on his face. And that was all there was. No lust, no wickedness.

'Well, thank you. I'm sorry to put you to the trouble.'

'No trouble. I have a duty of care towards my employees.'

For which she was grateful, but that fantasist part of her did wish for something more.

'You will come to the Panigiri?' she pressed.

'I'll do my very best to attend,' Xander promised. 'But my life is complicated.'

'Your friends on the island will be devastated if you don't attend.'

'Thanks for making it easy for me,' he said wryly.

'I didn't mean to put pressure on you.'

'Didn't you?'

'All right,' she admitted. 'Maybe a little.' At which point Xander smiled, which was a rare and precious thing, she guessed. 'Everyone's life is complicated,' she said frankly, 'and this island has suffered more than it should. The children have been working for months—'

'Okay, okay, I get the message.'

'So, will you come?'

The islanders had left in droves when Achilles was in charge. Praxos would die if they didn't get this right and bring the people back home again. Xander had to see how much he meant to everyone, and how his presence at the Panigiri would give them confidence in the stability of the island going forward.

'I really can't guarantee anything,' he said flatly as he turned his ruggedly handsome face up to the sky.

'Because?' she pressed, determined not to let him off the hook.

The power of his stare, even in the dark, was riveting. 'Because Eleni and Romanos did a much better job than I could ever do,' he bit out. 'They devoted themselves to this island—'

'Why can't you?'

'Don't you ever tire of challenging me?'

'I feel very deeply about this.'

'I would never have guessed. May I take it that's the end of your lecture for tonight?'

'Not quite. I should add that we all run the same risk

of things we care about being taken away from us, but we have to go on. What else can we do?'

'Giving up clearly isn't your thing, Kyria Boom.'

'Rosy,' she said softly.

Was she finally getting through to him? She was taking quite a risk, confronting her boss over and over again, but if she didn't hold him to account, who would?

'Okay, then, Rosy. I'll see what I can do.'

'That's all I can ask.'

'For now,' he guessed, but there was a new note in his voice that warmed and encouraged her, because it almost sounded like humour. Far from giving her the creeps like Achilles, Xander had allowed her a glimpse of another side of him, and she couldn't stop her mind from racing on, to wonder what he'd be like if all his barriers were broken down. And it was just a short step from there to imagining the consequences if she could lose her own hang-ups at the same time. But as theirs was strictly a working relationship, she forced herself to put it out of her mind.

They parted at the entrance to the guesthouse, where Xander waited until she was safely inside. Not that there were any bogeymen on Praxos, now Achilles had gone, but she appreciated his care and courtesy and couldn't resist turning around to watch him walk away. She felt certain that if Xander stayed on the island Praxos would repay him by easing his sense of loss, and giving him an anchor in the hectic swirl of his life.

And she wanted him to stay.

There were good people in this world and there were

bad and, for all his rampant good looks and hair-raising reputation, Xander Tsakis had unexpectedly made her feel safe tonight.

CHAPTER FOUR

XANDER WOKE IN a foul mood, glared into his bathroom mirror and cursed. Why had he given Rosy such an impossible task? She had proved herself as a schoolteacher, and proved herself again by forging a successful bartering system that had saved the island when Achilles had done his best to drive Praxos into the sea, but did she have the savvy and the experience to handle an event as complex and as costly as the type of Panigiri he had in mind? Romanos had begged him to hold onto her. Had he just made that impossible? Would she leave if she felt she'd disappointed everyone?

He'd hardly slept that night for turning these things over in his mind. Missing Eleni and Romanos was still a raw wound, and in the darkness of the night it had seemed that the only way to heal that wound was to put distance between himself and all the happy memories they'd shared. That would mean leaving Praxos as soon as he could, but the more he thought about Rosy and what he'd asked her to do, the more sure he was that he must stay to oversee everything.

Oversee everything, or oversee Rosy? In spite of his dour mood, he smiled at the thought of her challenging gaze—and her incredible breasts to himself. The smile stayed with him as he headed for the bathroom and an ice-cold shower.

A ping on his phone brought him up short before he reached the door. A text from Rosy lifted his spirits even more. She was in control and motoring on—with or without him. She'd sent an invitation to the first meeting of the Panigiri committee, which would be held *prompt* at twelve o'clock that day.

He shook his head with an ironic laugh at her use of the word *prompt*. Was there nothing this woman wouldn't dare to do?

'I'll be there,' he warned her out loud.

The islanders gathered around the school gave him the warmest of greetings. This was the first time he'd appreciated the mark Rosy had made on Praxos. The sense of community, optimism and purpose was down to the woman at the hub of this and, as if to confirm his opinion, Alexa, the elderly headmistress Achilles had thrown on the scrap heap, hurried to his side to say, 'We're going to have the best Panigiri ever with Rosy at the helm. Your parents would have been proud of everything she has achieved, but the island is your responsibility now.'

'And one I take seriously,' he assured the redoubtable senior. 'Your back wages will be paid, with a generous bonus—'

'I don't need a bonus,' Kyria Christos assured him. 'Working with Rosy is reward enough.'

He turned to look for Rosy in the crowd, but not before he caught sight of Kyria Christos's conspiratorial wink. What was she up to now? Whenever one of the seniors on the island came up with a plan, everyone else had better beware.

'Check your bank account when you get home,' he reminded her, before yielding to his hunting instinct and heading off.

'Kyrie Tsakis!' Rosy exclaimed. 'You did come to the meeting after all.'

'Xander,' he reminded her. 'Of course I'm here. I wouldn't miss this.'

Her expression was dubious, but he didn't care because her intoxicating scent more than made up for it. That, together with flashing emerald eyes and lush breasts, once again trapped beneath her clothing, this time a sensible shirt. Rosy Boom was the most appealing woman he'd ever met, which surprised him, bearing in mind the beauties he usually dated. But their beauty was plastic and fake, he decided, and they had empty, dull eyes compared to Rosy's bright, enthusiastic ones. It would be the easiest thing in the world to lean forward and kiss her, but not in front of this audience or rumours would fly. He must only see Rosy Boom as Romanos had seen her, as an asset Praxos could not afford to lose, and nothing else.

'Shall we?' she said, making her way through the crowd. When she swivelled around to check he was following, he felt her gaze like a soft, glancing blow. 'Are you here to volunteer,' she pressed with her usual frankness, 'or are you just here to observe?'

'I'm following your instruction to attend a meeting at noon,' he teased straight-faced.

She laughed at that. 'I wouldn't call it an instruction,

and there's still plenty of time before the meeting for you to volunteer your services.'

'Isn't my money enough?'

This earned him a long, steady stare. 'Money isn't the answer to everything, you know,' she said quietly.

He raised a cynical brow. 'So what role do you think I'm best suited to?'

She pretended to think about this for a moment. 'Well, there's a lot of heavy lifting to be done.'

When was there not? he mused as she forged on through the crowd.

'I saw you swimming in the sea this morning,' she informed him when they reached the table where the volunteers would sit. 'You swim very well,' she added, but her cheeks had suddenly turned red.

Hmm. He'd decided to swim naked this morning.

And now she looked decidedly uncomfortable. What had happened to Rosy Boom, to make her so wary of men?

'How close were you?' he asked, trying to make light of her reaction.

'Close enough.'

This time, she met his gaze as if to say, *I saw you naked, but no, I didn't run scared like a baby rabbit; I stood and admired you from a distance. But don't get ahead of yourself, because you were just another interesting sight on the beach.*

'Do you visit the beach every day?' he asked.

'I try to.'

'Then we may meet again.'

'Possibly.' She angled her head to stare up into his eyes. 'Do you swim?'

'Yes. Shall I call the meeting to order?' she suggested.

'Your meeting. Your call.' He held her stare for as long as was decent. Would she tell him what had put those shadows in her eyes?

Not today, he concluded as she banged her gavel on the table and all the chatter died. Anyone who thought Rosy Boom was a meek and mild mouse either lacked his Romani intuition or they didn't know her. Complex, yes, but she was hiding something from him. What that might be hijacked his thoughts throughout the meeting.

Rosy certainly had what it took to organise the Panigiri. In spite of their wretched treatment at the hands of Achilles, she had so many offers of help from the people. Who could resist Rosy's confidence that the island would recover? When the meeting ended he congratulated her, adding, 'You have an army of helpers. I doubt you'll need my help as well.'

'You're not getting away with it that easily. I can assure you that you are needed. *I* need you—' And just when he thought she'd said more than she'd intended, Rosy cocked her head to add cheekily, 'Who else will do the heavy lifting?'

'Good to know I'm useful for something,' he conceded in a lazy drawl.

'Xander?'

She was ready to go. 'May I escort you home?' he asked.

'You may,' she said with a regal tilt of her head.

That made him feel unusually pleased, even though he'd never had to ask a woman's permission before. They usually made themselves comfortable in whatever vehicle he had to hand, before he'd even had the chance to take his seat. Rosy was nothing like that, and his respect for her soared.

The meeting had gone even better than Rosy had hoped—apart from a flash of heat in Xander's eyes when they'd stared at each other afterwards. She'd had to tell herself that she was mistaken. Apart from feeling slightly foolish at imagining yet again that he was attracted to her, she wondered why the possibility hadn't alarmed her. He was so very different to Achilles. That seemed to be the answer. She could excuse herself for being wary of him because Xander had grown up alongside Achilles, but there wasn't a single iota of him that reminded her of his brother.

'You're leaving,' Alexa observed with a meaningful glance in Xander's direction.

'Taking the opportunity to talk some things through on the way home,' Rosy excused.

Give the seniors an inch and they'd take a mile; gossip would fly, and they'd have her married to Xander by the morning.

'Hey—are you coming?' she called over her shoulder to Xander. 'I meant to tell you,' she added when he strolled alongside her, 'but there wasn't a chance during the meeting. Your people have been amazing, offering all sorts of help—especially a man called Peter.'

'One of my PAs—prematurely grey, sharp as a tack, lean, but not mean, and endlessly helpful. That's Peter. You'll get to meet him in person very soon.'

'I look forward to it. I just have to make sure that your people don't take over, because the islanders are itching to help, and this is their home.'

'They are lucky to have you,' he admitted with a shrug of his powerful shoulders.

And, just like that, the meeting faded away, to be replaced by hard muscle beneath the soft-touch cotton of Xander's form-fitting shirt.

'Rosy?'

'Yes, I'm here,' she lied, preferring for once to linger inside the fantasy of mapping Xander's magnificent body beneath his relaxed casual shirt with her fingers and then her lips, rather than concentrate on everything they had accomplished that morning.

'You'll have my backing every step of the way.'

'Great. Thank you.'

'Now I've got you to myself—'

She flinched. She couldn't help herself.

'Can I ask you a personal question?'

'Yes,' she said uncertainly, wishing the sudden flashback of Achilles pressing her down on that desk would go away. She could still smell the foul stench of his breath in her mind.

'Rosy? Are you okay?'

'Absolutely fine. Sorry, I was just thinking of something else, and…'

'And?' Xander pressed.

'Oh, nothing. I'm just missing your parents, and the good times we had.'

'Which you will revive. I'm sure of it.'

'Thank you.'

When she stared into Xander's eyes she realised he had no intention of blurring the invisible line between them, which was that of boss and employee.

And she shouldn't even be thinking about it, wishing that could change.

'Thanks for the back wages. They landed in everyone's bank accounts this morning.'

'Don't thank me. You were owed that money. It will never happen again.'

He found it easy to talk about business, but what about Xander's emotional commitment to the island? Would he stay, or had there been too much grief to bear?

'You must see the difference when you're here—how you lift everyone?'

'I can't see the difference when I'm not here.'

Was that a glint of humour? If so, it was a huge step forward, and one she couldn't let go.

'You're the anchor for the islanders, and their inspiration. They believe you're the only man who can walk in Romanos's shoes—'

Xander's face darkened. 'No one can ever hope to do that.'

'But you're the closest thing they have to him, so please don't let them down.'

His expression blackened even more. 'If anyone else spoke to me as you do—'

'You'd hear the truth every day of your life,' Rosy stated firmly.

With a shake of his head, Xander conceded with the faintest hint of a smile.

Rosy's fresh wildflower scent had invaded his senses, and to distract himself he reached for the stack of papers and the briefcase she was carrying.

'Thanks. You know I'd happily work here for nothing,' she said, gazing around as a warm breeze freed shining tendrils of hair from her severe up-do to coil on her brow and her neck.

'Hopefully, that won't be necessary.' He had to rip his gaze away from the tender, kissable nape of her neck as they moved off. 'You've more than proved your loyalty to the island by carrying on working without a wage.'

'My work with the children is worth far more than money,' she said, frowning. 'For me, the Panigiri is a tribute to your parents, and I'm sure in time you'll leave a similar legacy.'

Eleni and Romanos had given him more than money. He could see that now, and it stung to have Rosy point it out to him. Why had he not seen this before? Because the climb out of that gutter had been long and hard, and somehow, in spite of the selfless love he'd received from Eleni and Romanos, he'd never stopped running.

Rosy had ventured where none dared to go, shining a spotlight on the fact that his business mind ruled everything he did, because that way he didn't have to engage his feelings and risk getting hurt. His early life had knocked all warmer, gentler emotions out of him. Protecting himself in that way had saved him in so many ways, allowing him to concentrate on the practicalities of life, like not freezing to death, or starving. He supposed now that he'd never got out of the habit of focusing on the practical. Look how rich it had made him. He'd had no reason to change.

No one had ever talked to him as Rosy did. Nor should she, really, if they were to keep the line between boss and employee intact.

'I won't let you off the hook,' she promised, distracting him from his uneasy thoughts. 'You can leave me here,' she added as they approached the white picket fence that marked out the guesthouse garden. 'Before you go—I wanted to say thanks for turning up to the meeting, and thanks again for carrying everything home for me.'

'Is that all I'm good for?' he teased as she claimed her belongings.

'Time will tell,' she said with a slanting smile and mischief in her eyes that tightened his groin to the point of pain.

For a few potent seconds neither of them moved, then Rosy blushed as if she thought he was going to kiss her. He'd like to do a lot more than that, but something hinted at some trouble in her past, perhaps related to a man. And he couldn't forget that he was her boss; their circumstances were all wrong for any kind of liaison, and he was glad when she stepped away.

'When I've dropped these off and freshened up a bit, I'm going back to the school to clear up,' she explained. 'See you tomorrow, same time, same place?'

'Possibly,' he murmured, lost in thought.

'Possibly?' she repeated with one brow raised.

'Yeah,' he confirmed as their eyes met in a long, challenging look.

Was Rosy too good to be true? Eleni and Romanos had showered love on him, but he only had to look around to know how special they were. People changed like shifting sand, and the scars of his early life had never left him. With his particular situation in life, the massive wealth and the significance of the Tsakis family name, was it any wonder he was cynical of people's motives?

* * *

Would Xander turn up for the meeting tomorrow or not? Rosy wondered as she hurried back to the school later that afternoon. Just when she thought she was getting to know him a little better, he brought the shutters down and closed her out. Maybe the sun had addled her brain? She had thought for one mad moment, when he'd left her at the guesthouse, that maybe he'd wanted to kiss her. Not maybe—definitely, she concluded. Xander Tsakis was a decisive man. If he had wanted to kiss her, she'd have known about it. And she'd wanted it too.

So, her cynical self demanded, *you think Xander Tsakis finds you attractive? The same man who usually has a supermodel hanging on his arm?*

Had she ever seen him with a down-to-earth woman whose hair refused to be tamed, and whose idea of high fashion was a clean shirt? No. And it was never going to happen.

Having answered these questions to her satisfaction, Rosy entered the school, only to find everything was already straight again. Alexa must have beaten her to it. So she kicked off her sandals and set off home across the beach. She couldn't stop thinking about Xander, and that sensual, brooding expression in his eyes. Curious that she felt so safe with him, when his swarthy, rampantly masculine good looks made him appear far more dangerous than Achilles. Scrunching her toes in the cool, damp sand, she could only think that Achilles had been a sneak, a weak man who preyed on others, while Xander was the anchor this island needed.

And you? What do you need? that annoying part of her asked.

'Hey—' Catching sight of Alexa taking a shortcut home across the sand, she hurried to catch up with her friend. 'Thanks for tidying everything up. You should have waited for me.'

Alexa smiled and gave her a wink. 'You had more important things to do. You do know Panigiri is the traditional time to hunt for a husband on Praxos?'

Rosy heaved a theatrical sigh. 'I have no idea what you mean.' But she had made it her business to know all the local customs.

'This is your chance to make sure you have someone to cuddle up to when the nights grow cold.'

'I have a perfectly good hot-water bottle, thank you very much. It gives me no trouble and never answers back.'

'You shouldn't be single at your age.'

'At my age? I'm only twenty-four.'

They both knew Rosy's past was littered with setbacks and grief. She hadn't the time or the inclination to think about romance. And then Achilles had knocked all thoughts of striking up any type of relationship with a man out of her for good. Or so she'd thought, until his adoptive brother had suddenly appeared on the scene. But what use was being attracted to Xander Tsakis when he belonged firmly in the realms of fantasy? She'd do far better to concentrate on her work at the school.

'Then let me put this another way,' Alexa said, catching hold of Rosy's arm to drive her point home. 'Don't allow what happened with Achilles to turn you off men.'

They'd never mentioned it after the event, and for

Alexa to speak of it now came as a shock to Rosy, but it was only fair to set her friend straight.

'Don't worry, I'm not about to make a fool of myself with a man like Xander Tsakis.'

'A fool?' Alexa echoed, pressing her lips down in disapproval. 'You're no fool, and neither is Xander. Just wait until the Panigiri works its magic.'

'And pigs start to fly?' Rosy teased.

'Ti?' Alexa queried with a frown.

'An old English saying. Just ignore me,' Rosy begged, linking arms with her as they crossed the sand.

But Alexa wasn't in the mood for ignoring anything. 'Just wait until the dancing starts,' she confided. 'You won't be able to resist him then—'

'I shall do my best,' Rosy said firmly.

'I predict you'll dance through the night.'

'With my two left feet?'

'Don't worry—Xander will teach you everything you need to know.'

'About traditional Greek dancing?' Rosy thought it wise to add. She was sure there were a lot of other things he could teach her, but—

'Xander!' He'd come down the cliff path and was standing right in front of her. 'I thought you'd gone home,' she gasped.

'Did I overhear you refusing to dance with me, Kyria Boom?'

She gazed around but Alexa had slipped away, leaving Rosy without her dependable chaperone. Faced by a deeply tanned titan with an unruly mop of inky-black hair and a physique to rival a gladiator, she was forced to answer his question. 'What if I did?'

'I would have to persuade you that you've made a mistake.'

What form would that persuasion take? Slipping away into dreamland was temptingly easy. How could any man make her feel so safe yet look so dangerous? The lift of one sweeping brow was all it took for her body to yearn for things that were completely out of the question.

'You shouldn't be eavesdropping,' she scolded lightly. 'You'll never hear good of yourself.'

Xander shrugged. 'I'll take my chances.'

Was this a game for him, and Rosy just another casual roll of the dice? She had thought she was getting to know a more complex individual than the media suggested, but she couldn't ignore the indisputable fact that Xander's reputation as a playboy was legendary. She only had to see that dangerous laughter in his eyes to know there was truth in the rumours.

Turning to safer thoughts, she said with an equally careless shrug of her shoulders, 'We can all dance and feast at the Panigiri—'

'Just not us, together?' he queried dryly.

How could she answer that? She walked on ahead, expecting him to catch up and walk alongside her, but when she eventually turned to look there was no sign of Xander. Now she was disappointed he'd walked away? Rosy's mouth twisted in a rueful line. If their association, friendship—she didn't even know what to call it—was nothing more than a game for Xander, it was time to learn the rules.

CHAPTER FIVE

Successful meeting followed successful meeting until finally Rosy declared her arrangements for the Panigiri complete. Xander had heard about this from Maria, who'd said that if everything went as smoothly as the team deserved Rosy would have accomplished the seemingly impossible, which was to give something really special back to the islanders who had suffered so much under Achilles. The event would be much bigger than previous years, but no less warm and welcoming. The Rosy touch, he acknowledged.

No one should have suffered on the island while he was away. And no one would suffer now he was back. Manoeuvring his favourite Lamborghini through the busy centre of town, he felt a renewed sense of urgency to make things right as he headed to the final sign-off meeting with Rosy and the team.

Romanos had impressed upon him that to understand Panigiri was to understand all human passion. Romanos would have been proud of what Rosy, his young protégée, had achieved. Even Xander was surprised at how fast she'd got things moving. He wasn't easily given to an excess of emotion, not surprising when in his early life anything other than mute compliance could earn him a slap in the face from one of the pimps, but today he'd felt a surge of admiration for Rosy.

She was a survivor like him, and so determined to help after Achilles had done his best to destroy everything. He grimaced at the memory of his brother. As a child, it had sickened him to witness those who took advantage of others weaker than themselves. He had vowed then that when he grew older he would make sure he was in a position to make a difference. Romanos and Eleni had set him on the road, but with their passing he had already started slipping back to his old, suspicious ways. He'd always made sure that the women he was with knew the score, and he had never felt the need to invite one of their number to Praxos. He had chosen to live his life without complications or distractions, and that same unswerving focus had allowed him to develop his commercial interests into a multi-billion-dollar conglomerate.

That didn't keep him warm at night, though, did it?

It kept countless families warm at night instead, he argued fiercely with himself.

And then a call came through.

Parking up, he listened intently. Grinding his jaw, he cut the call short. He'd heard everything he needed to. A competitor was sniffing around one of his business interests, threatening employees' livelihoods. Xander was needed to straighten things out, but that would mean leaving Praxos and missing the festival. The thought of disappointing the islanders, after all they'd suffered, made it hard to leave, but that was what he must do, because the employees at his threatened company mattered too.

This year's Panigiri marked a new beginning for Praxos. If he missed it, there'd be no getting it back. How would Rosy feel if he upped and left—that he couldn't be trusted? His word was his bond. He'd never allowed anything to stand in the way of business before, because those interests funded the island as well as his charitable concerns. If he left now it would seem that he didn't care enough about the island to stay.

Stuck between a rock and a hard place, he decided to pack, go, and come back as fast as possible.

And leave his PA Peter to break the news to Rosy?

After working for Xander for many years, Peter knew how to be diplomatic.

What the actual hell?

Rosy stared at Xander's quietly spoken PA in shocked surprise. 'Kyrie Tsakis won't be available to open the Panigiri? I don't understand.' Last-minute details banged in her brain. 'And he's waited until now to tell me?'

She stared out towards the crowd, already gathered at the foot of the stage, waiting eagerly for Xander to speak. Everything was poised and ready. The parade had formed, bands were tuning their instruments, children's faces were wreathed in excited smiles. How could Xander do this to them all, when he'd seemed so enthusiastic, so engaged, and as keen as anyone else to turn a new page for the island? His decision left her feeling gutted—literally gutted, like some hapless fish sliced from head to tail with its emotions hanging out for all to see.

When it came down to it, turned out Xander was as selfish as Achilles, and that hurt.

Gathering herself, she forced a reassuring smile for the audience before turning away from the mic to face Xander's PA. 'Kyrie Tsakis is supposed to be giving a speech to mark the opening of the festival.'

'And he will,' Peter assured her.

'By video link?' Rosy guessed with exasperation. 'What type of message does that send to the islanders? I care about what you've been through, but not enough to be here with you today, sharing the joy of this new start for Praxos?'

'Kyrie Tsakis has been called away on business, but has left a generous donation—'

'A generous donation?' Rosy repeated with disgust. 'Money alone can't provide what Praxos needs. Doesn't he realise what he means to everyone—what he symbolises? Continuity. Stability. Doesn't he care about Romanos's legacy? I'm sorry,' she added, reining herself in. 'I know this isn't your fault, but—'

Turning, she ground her jaw and fought to regain her composure. Why attend all the meetings, making everyone think he cared about them? Rosy felt duped, and was sure everyone else would feel the same. Her friends had invested so much hope in this opening ceremony, and now it was ruined.

So, sort it out!

'Please tell Kyrie Tsakis,' she told his PA politely, 'that we don't need his recorded message. I will ask the school's headmistress, Alexa Christos, to speak on his behalf. After all, it was she who made today possible—'

'You made today possible.'

'Xander?' Rosy exclaimed, reeling with shock.

Romanos and Rosy... Rosy and Romanos. No one on earth could change his plans, but they had. He'd never done anything like this before. He hated delegating, but on this occasion he'd sent his best legal team to handle the company problem. Letting the islanders down was wrong. He knew what Romanos would have done. Letting Rosy down, after the way she'd organised everything and all the hard work she'd put in, would be churlish. If he was known for anything it was showing respect and gratitude to his employees, so why should Rosy be any different?

Indicating that his PA could leave them, he took his first decisive step in making sure that Praxos would have the celebration it deserved. And then he could leave with a clear conscience.

Rosy stood proud beneath his scrutiny. He didn't blame her for not gushing her thanks at his last-minute appearance when he'd just put her through the mill. Wearing traditional Greek costume, she couldn't have looked more beautiful. The white dress was simple but suited her. Everything suited Rosy. With its wide sleeves and colourful apron, it was the sash at her waist in particular that caught his attention. Painstakingly cross-stitched in red, he guessed by the children, he knew instinctively that every stitch had been sewn with love. No high-class couturier could hope to compete with that. Her glorious hair was partially covered by a simple white lace headscarf and the outfit was completed with a flame-red bolero jacket, heavily ornamented in sequins and gold thread. This last was a treasured heir-loom that Eleni used to wear. Kept in a locked glass case in the Town Hall, this precious garment only ever made an appearance during Panigiri. Alexa had used to wear the gold coin necklace currently jingling around Rosy's neck, which was yet another symbol of the island's love for a woman who had battled alongside them during some very dark days.

'Are you going to stare at me for much longer?' She'd obviously recovered from the shock of seeing him when she added, 'Are you going to deliver this speech of yours, or would you just prefer to wave to your adoring crowd and leave?'

He couldn't blame her for that dig either.

Her breasts heaved with emotion. Picking up the mic, he announced, 'Welcome, everyone! Welcome to this start of a new era on Praxos!'

The cheers were deafening, but when he turned to face Rosy he saw the urgent questions in her eyes. Covering the mic, he told her briskly, 'Business can wait.'

'But not for ever,' she guessed shrewdly.

He couldn't argue with that. After all, Praxos itself depended on his commercial interests to survive and prosper, as Romanos would have wanted.

'Anyway, at least you're here,' she said with a fixed smile that failed to mask the hurt in her eyes.

Turning away again, he spoke the words the crowd had been waiting for. 'This year's Panigiri is officially open!'

Rosy couldn't deny that having Xander at the celebration lifted everything. It would have gone smoothly without him, she would have made sure of that, but he was one of those lucky few who could add lustre to any event.

And her heart? Her heart was thundering just at the sight of him. With his wild black hair, sharp black stubble, dark clothing, rugged boots and leather wristbands, Xander Tsakis radiated glamour and danger in equal measure. He'd better not let these people down or she'd never forgive him.

'Just in case you're in any doubt,' he was saying to a group of admirers clustered around him, 'I have this woman to thank for making today possible.'

Me?

'Rosy, come over here...'

'It was a team effort,' she assured everyone. 'I've had loads of help from so many of you.'

'What you have achieved in such a short time is significant,' Xander argued to a chorus of murmured assent.

'You did the heavy lifting,' she reminded him dryly, still not quite ready to forgive him for his last-minute appearance. If what his PA had said was any indication of the truth, he'd be leaving as soon as he could anyway.

'This is as close to a professional event as any I've seen,' Xander told her as they left the stage together.

Think what she might about organising an event, or Xander being here, when she'd thought he wouldn't come, all her body seemed to care about was that they were walking side by side, his hand a hair's breadth from her own.

'Thank you,' she said huskily with a betraying dry throat.

She felt the power of Xander's stare as he turned to

look at her, and covered her chest with one hand, where her pouting breasts were exposed to his view beneath the flimsy white top of her outfit.

'Yes, you had help,' he said in a dispassionate tone, apparently not noticing the fact that her nipples were now standing proudly to attention. 'But the fact remains that you were the driving force.' While Xander was the undeniable force wreaking havoc on her hard-won control. 'What I've seen so far,' he continued smoothly, 'has really impressed me—' She gasped out loud as their hands brushed. 'Forgive me,' he said, stepping aside to put more distance between them. 'I can't imagine what all this has cost. If you need more money to settle the accounts, just say so. I'm happy to pay—'

'Everything's paid for,' she explained in a strangled tone, feeling as if some strange force was driving them together. 'Haven't you seen my latest spreadsheet? Too busy?' she couldn't help suggesting.

That lazy black stare was scrambling her brain cells, acting like a magnet, keeping her gaze locked on his face. But even then she could feel his stare warming her breasts.

It didn't even come as a surprise when he murmured, 'Amazing...'

'We don't need any more money,' she said sharply in an attempt to return things to an even keel. 'The amount you deposited in the bank was more than enough. Actually, it proved to be totally unnecessary.'

'How could that be?' Suddenly, he was all business again.

'Most of the performers, the services, the music,

come from Praxos, and the islanders refused to accept payment.'

'What about the pony rides for the children?' he pressed as they passed a line of ponies with colourful ribbons threaded through their plaited manes and tails.

The power of his stare on her face was like a scorching brand, demanding answers.

'The Acostas,' she squeaked.

She squeaked? What the hell was happening to her? Xander Tsakis was happening to her, Rosy accepted as her body yearned and her mind screamed, *No!*

'What?' he all but exploded. 'Tell me you didn't ask the Acostas for money!'

'They insisted on paying for anything horse-related. When I contacted their team office, they said you were always generous with their charities, and they were glad to have an opportunity to pay you back.'

Xander made a sound halfway between a growl and an indignant sigh. 'You do seem to have worked a miracle,' he finally admitted. 'But I don't approve of calling in favours.'

She frowned. 'Hasn't this island suffered enough because of pride?'

'I sincerely hope you're not comparing me to my brother?'

As they faced off, she remembered Xander's first day back on Praxos, when they'd met at the school. She had felt threatened, in case he was like Achilles. *Would he press her down on the desk too? Could she rely on fate to save her again?*

All these thoughts had gone through her head as she'd relived the repulsive touch of Achilles' sweaty palms on her thighs and his bruising grip on her arms, and imagined she could still smell his stale breath. She'd felt so helpless, so fearful of Achilles—

'Rosy?' Xander's voice broke into her distressed thoughts. He'd brought his face close to hers, and his breath was warm and minty, as he startled her into meeting the genuine concern in his eyes. 'Are you okay?' he asked.

'I'm fine,' she lied with a smile. 'There's still so much to show you. Perhaps we should move on?'

Xander doubted Rosy was fine. She had paled at the mention of his brother. What was going on? It was too late to do anything about him now, but he could at least make sure that Achilles' wrongs were never repeated by anyone else. Security was just one aspect he intended to tighten on the island.

'You're nothing like your brother,' Rosy said out of the blue.

'I'm pleased to hear it.' So her reaction was something to do with Achilles, he thought grimly. He badly wanted to ask her to explain, but it was up to Rosy to confide in him, if she wanted to.

'Back to the money,' he said briskly. 'We'll go through the spreadsheets together, but— *Camels?*' he exclaimed.

'Thanks to your friend, Sheikh Shahin,' Rosy revealed, smiling.

Conjuring up an image of his strikingly good-looking friend, he could only grind his jaw as he imagined Shahin's conversation with Rosy.

'How's he involved in this?'

'I read an article where he mentioned you, and how generous you'd been to his charities—'

'So you got in touch with him?' Incredulity coloured his every word.

'With his office,' Rosy revealed. 'But the Sheikh insisted on speaking to me personally once he heard what I wanted, and he was absolutely charming—'

Unaccountable rage pooled inside him. 'I'm sure he was.' Shahin was single, and a notorious player.

Was he jealous of his friend's interest in Rosy? This had never happened before.

You've never cared enough before, that incredibly annoying voice taunted him.

'You haven't met Shahin, have you?' he asked warily. 'You just spoke to him on the phone?'

'Online,' Rosy revealed. 'There's no need to worry. Shahin was amazing. He made all the arrangements and paid for everything.'

'Someone else to be indebted to?' he grumbled.

'You're on an equal footing, from what Shahin told me. He's one of your greatest admirers.'

'I'm sure he is.' If Xander could provide a woman as fascinating as Rosy for Shahin to chat to, he was almost certainly at the top of his friend's list. With a sound of exasperation, he strode off, leaving Rosy to hurry after him.

'Camels aside,' he called back to her, 'I don't know how on earth you paid for all this.'

'I can account for every penny,' she assured him, coming alongside him.

His disbelieving hum prompted Rosy to take him on.

'Do you ever wonder if your obsession with money is the reason you're still alone?'

Incredulous, he stopped dead. Spinning around to face her, he fired back, 'I don't recall inviting your personal observation on my marital state.'

'Just as well,' she muttered.

'I'm sorry, I didn't quite catch that.'

'You're alone,' she repeated firmly. 'Having no one to come home to can't be easy.'

'So, now you feel sorry for me?' he growled.

'No. We usually get what we deserve from life.'

Her bluntness infuriated him, but he couldn't argue with what she'd said. The race to put as much distance as he could between his early years and the here and now might well have blinded him to everything but the accumulation of wealth. Money had allowed him to fulfil his childish dreams and ambitions, and if he could also use it to fund charitable projects like the one he'd set up to help homeless children all across Greece, and to save Praxos when Achilles had almost destroyed the island, then so much the better.

Rosy was still staring at him as if she expected him to say something in his own defence. He would not do that. It was bad enough she'd made him face the past, and how vulnerable he'd been as a child, with her words. He was strong now, and he vowed he would never be weak again. Money was the only certainty in life. It was far more reliable than love. People were often unpredictable, but he could always count on cash.

They had reached the outskirts of the celebrations, where the cobbled streets of the town gave way to narrow passageways leading to the shore. Suddenly, he felt a longing for the cooling wash of the sea. That never failed to restore order to his mind.

'I'd better get back to the celebrations,' Rosy said as the sounds of the sea grew louder.

'No. Stay—'

But she'd gone, like a will-o'-the-wisp, slipping away on the offshore breeze. She should stay away—well away from him. Rosy was an exceptional woman who deserved a man who would love and cherish her; a man who would devote his life to making her happy, and who understood the value of love. Xander would never expose himself to that sort of risk. Losing Romanos and Eleni was the final straw. He would willingly spend the rest of his life to work that gave others the chance of a better future.

What about his own future?

In spite of Rosy's observations, he saw no reason to change. The way he lived now suited him very well. Didn't it?

CHAPTER SIX

HE TOOK HIS TIME to stroll back to the town square, where he could see Rosy still circulating, making sure everyone was having a great time.

'Do you ever sit down?' he called out, catching hold of her arm as she was about to whirl past him.

'Do you?' she countered.

'I trust you'll make yourself available when the dancing starts?'

A spark of humour flared in her eyes. 'Is that your way of asking me to dance?'

'Would I dare?'

Her gaze found his lips. 'Oh, I think you would.'

'And as I don't see anyone else asking—'

'Short of a partner, Xander?' And with that, she pulled away.

'No, but I'd like to dance with you,' he called after her, wondering when he'd ever had to beg a woman to dance with him before. The answer, of course, was, never.

'You must be desperate,' Rosy yelled over her shoulder with a grin that gave him hope.

If there was anything he loved more in this world

than the hunt he couldn't think what that might be right now.

'See you later.'

'Maybe,' she shouted back at him.

Maybe? Romanos and Eleni had always made a point of waiting on their guests, and it was an honour to carry on that tradition, but they'd also always opened the dancing, and his plan had been to do that with Rosy.

Was she going to hide away to avoid dancing with Xander? Didn't she trust herself to dance with him? Rosy couldn't resist casting another glance his way. Could anyone turn down the chance to be wrapped in those powerful arms, or be pressed up tight against that warm, hard body? If she risked it, could she trust her own body to behave? It hadn't done too well so far. Didn't matter how sensible she was, her body was a dangerous, wilful thing. Xander didn't frighten her. She frightened herself. Her terrifying encounter with Achilles in the schoolroom was nothing like being with Xander. Achilles hadn't needed any encouragement to assault her, while Xander remained elusive in a way that made butterflies flutter in her stomach and fantasies lodge in her head.

Fortunately, she didn't have too much time to think about it before the band was due to strike up. She still had to announce the results of the silent auction. She'd never run one before, but it seemed fairly straightforward, with sealed bids for each prize and the highest bid winning the lot. The prizes ran from baskets of fruit, grown on the island, to a dinner cooked by Rosy. There was even a swish SUV generously donated by the Acosta family, and a diamond necklace from Sheikh Shahin, as well as a holiday in his rapidly developing desert kingdom. Xander had been more than generous, offering to pay college fees for an island child. What the islanders didn't know was that Rosy was under strict instructions to award his prize to the smallest bid, rather than the largest.

The auction was a huge success, and by the time it came to the last lot, which was for the dinner cooked by herself, she made everyone laugh as she promised to buy a meal in rather than subject the winner to her cooking. Opening the envelope to reveal the winner, she was interrupted by a familiar husky male voice calling from the crowd, 'I bid a million euros.'

As a stunned silence fell, she called back to Xander, 'Are you sure you're brave enough?'

'I am,' he confirmed.

'In that case, I accept your bid.'

As laughter and cheers rang out, Xander mounted the stage to stand at her side. With a bone-melting glance Rosy's way, he assured the crowd, 'This is going to be worth every euro cent.'

What on earth had she been thinking offering to cook a meal? A cordon bleu chef she was not. Batch cooking at the guesthouse was as far as it went. Cooking for a billionaire accustomed to high-end everything could only be a disappointment.

'Cheese sandwich?' she suggested.

More laughter and cheering, but then she remembered Xander's appalling childhood, when it was said he'd been forced to rifle through dustbins to find enough to eat, and her heart squeezed at the image. As her cheeks fired red, he put a firm hand on her arm as he led her off the stage.

'And now we dance,' he murmured.

'You're very sure of yourself.'

'Yes, I am.'

'A million times over.'

He smiled a crooked smile that made her pulse quicken. 'I would like my money's worth.'

'Dream on.' She laughed a little nervously.

'Hey, look,' Xander said, bringing his face so close to hers that Rosy's cheeks tingled. 'I think the children have something for you...'

Alexa, who was shepherding her charges, exchanged a broad wink with Xander. What was going on now?

'Is this a set-up?'

'No,' Xander reassured her. 'This is the crowning of the Queen of the Panigiri.'

'What? Me?'

'I can't think of anyone more deserving.'

When their eyes locked this time she saw the glow of humour, as well as heat of a very different kind. Then one of the children stepped forward with a wreath of fresh flowers in her hand, and as the others formed a horseshoe around Rosy, Alexa called out, 'I will now ask Xander Tsakis to crown the Queen of the Panigiri...'

Seeing the faces of the children beaming with happiness and anticipation, Rosy knew she had to do whatever they wanted.

Even bow her head to Xander Tsakis?

Even that.

Once her headscarf was removed and she was crowned, he was insistent they open the dancing.

'Be gentle with me,' he said as they approached the dance floor.

'Shouldn't that be the other way around?'

He shrugged and smiled a smile that made her pulse go crazy. But was he just doing this out of a sense of obligation? She knew Eleni and Romanos had always opened the dancing so, as their successor, Xander was just doing his duty and she was convenient. But the moment his big fist closed around her hand she didn't care about formalities. All that mattered was this, for as long as it lasted.

The first dance passed in a dream, and then more couples joined them on the dance floor, ready to take part in a traditional Greek dance. This began with slow, deliberate steps that quickly speeded up to calls of *'Opa!'* Dancing with Xander was an education in temptation. Greek men were sexy, and he was off the scale hot. While she was just a red-headed schoolteacher with freckles and flowers in her hair, Rosy reminded herself.

So let's not get ahead of ourselves.

That didn't stop erotic thoughts bombarding her mind while they danced.

Rosy moved like a dream, and picked up the steps so quickly she might have been Greek. The music had an elemental beat which suited his savage mood. Did Rosy feel the same sense of awareness growing between them? For once, his sixth sense remained silent. She was so different to any woman he'd known—she was impossible to read.

When the dance roared to its inevitable conclusion, she clung onto him, laughing as she exclaimed breathlessly, 'That was *amazing*! But can we find somewhere quiet to recover?'

Any other woman and he would have taken that as a euphemism for, *Where's your bedroom?* But Rosy clearly meant exactly what she said.

'Somewhere quiet,' he agreed, leading her away from the dance floor into the shadows beyond.

What he had not expected was that Rosy would stand on her tiptoes to drop the briefest of kisses on his mouth.

'That's to say thank you,' she explained. 'For your donations to the auction, and for the dance.'

'No need to thank me.' No need to explain anything. When had a woman made the first move before? Clutching and grabbing, yes—mostly for his wallet—but this was a kiss he would remember for ever.

When she went to step away, he pulled her back. She stared into his eyes, and then he slowly bent and brushed his lips against her mouth. Danger signs were everywhere. He ignored them. Emotions he'd banished for years threatened to show themselves and overwhelm him. Pushing them aside, he concentrated on Rosy, whose breathing had become erratic and whose hands were ever more demanding as she clutched his shoulders. Cupping her face in his hands, he deepened the kiss.

'You won't be needing these tonight,' he said gruffly as he took off her glasses.

'How will I find my way home?'

'You won't.'

'Ah,' she whispered as he led her away.

For this one night they were no longer boss and employee, but two people who, briefly, were better together than apart.

* * *

To her surprise, Rosy had no doubts about what she was doing, none at all. She couldn't explain why she felt safe with Xander, just that she did. He'd opened a door she had thought would be permanently closed after her run-in with Achilles. They were walking at speed, as if they were both impatient to do this. Would he care that she was still a virgin? Coming from the sophisticated world Xander inhabited, would he think her naive? Would he understand that she'd either been too busy with her studies for romance, or trying to make a new life for herself when everything had gone wrong at home? Not that there had been much temptation before—a few fumblings in the back seat of a car, perhaps, but nothing like this incredible night, she realised, as they ran up the steps of the Big House together, and Xander opened the impressive front door.

'Bed or no bed?' he prompted briskly.

'Oh, bed—' If they made it that far.

'Are you sure?'

As he pinned her against the wall, fists planted, powerful forearms caging her face, she felt her legs give way. Next thing she knew, Xander had swung her into his arms.

'You're so pragmatic,' she commented, thinking about all the romance novels she'd read, where the hero took the heroine on the stairs because they couldn't wait to reach his bed.

'Always,' Xander confirmed.

He wanted sex. She wanted sex. What was wrong with her?

Xander was making it clear that this would be sex

with no strings attached, and no emotion either. It hurt. Could she deal with such a businesslike transaction? If not, she'd better tell him now, while they were still at the foot of the stairs.

Pragmatic? No. The idea that he could be sensible or logical now was becoming increasingly impossible. Off-balance, yes, he would admit to that. He felt a driving passion to be with Rosy that he couldn't explain. The need to pleasure her was matched by the need to protect her. He could only liken it to two halves of the same entity meeting. But did she feel the same?

To anchor himself, he turned to the strongest bond they shared, as far as the rest of the world was concerned, which was, of course, the Panigiri, but with his senses raging, he leapt in too quickly with the admission that the success she'd made of the Panigiri had taken him by surprise.

Rosy frowned up at him. 'Did you think me incompetent?'

She spoke good-humouredly, but his lack of tact had clearly hurt her, and after all she'd done to make the event a success, that was the last thing he had intended.

'I think you're incredible,' he said honestly.

'Then…?' Her steady gaze remained locked on his face.

His only hesitation now was the consideration of his experience versus Rosy's inexperience.

'I don't want to rush you.'

'What if I want to be rushed?' she suggested.

'Then I would have to show you another way…'

They stood in silence for a moment, and then he

reached for her coronet of flowers and the precious gold-coin necklace. Gently removing them, he talked softly in his own language, while Rosy closed her eyes and sighed. Lacking his familiarity with eroticism, she was completely vulnerable, completely lovely.

'I thought you wanted to talk about the Panigiri,' she whispered.

'Only if that's what you want,' he murmured as he dropped kisses on her neck.

'I don't want to talk about anything,' she admitted, lifting her chin to smile into his eyes.

'Good, because I'm going to kiss you again...and this time I won't stop.'

Yes. Everything about this felt right to her. Why shouldn't she throw caution to the wind for just once in her life, and spend one night in his arms? If his reputation was anything to go by, Xander wouldn't be looking for a repeat, nor would he be staying much longer on Praxos as he had that emergency to deal with, so just this once she wanted to feel every powerful naked inch of him, pressed up hard against her body. Never having known a man in the fullest sense of the word, she longed for it to be Xander who introduced her to the type of pleasure she had only ever dreamed about.

'The plate-smashing,' Xander murmured when he lifted his head.

'I'm sorry...what?'

'It marks the end of the Panigiri and the expulsion of any lingering evil on Praxos. Goodness knows, the island needs that. I'll have to be there for that. But not yet,' he said with a glance at the sapphire dial on his steel diver's watch. 'There's still time.'

Rosy's jaw dropped. 'You factored that into your plans?'

With a husky laugh, Xander whispered, 'No comment,' as he swept her into his arms.

CHAPTER SEVEN

THIS WAS A one-time deal, Xander told himself. He didn't do repeats. Yet again, Rosy surprised him, by winding her arms firmly around him as he steadied her on her feet beside his bed. Something told him not to take this final step with her unless he was ready to meet his match, but he'd always been a risk-taker; it was what accounted for his meteoric success in business.

'Kiss me,' she demanded, emerald fire blazing in her eyes.

'Just that?'

'To begin with,' she amended.

He removed the little jacket she wore carefully, by which time her eyes had darkened to black, with just the slimmest rim of jade around the pupils.

'Don't treat me as if I'm made of rice paper—'

'I won't. There isn't time.' His bedroom windows were open, a reminder that the party was still going full swing, but they still needed longer than they had. He'd have to take what he could get. Settling her on the bed, he stretched out beside her.

'And?' she said.

'Are you complaining?' Resting his chin on the heel of his hand, he stared at her with amusement.

'You bet I am.'

Bringing her close, he buried his face in her hair to inhale her delicious wildflower scent. Rosy had bewitched him. Sifting the silken skeins of her fiery hair through his fingers and then stroking her cheeks, her throat, he luxuriated in the warm, velvety texture of her skin. She was exquisite, but it was her honesty that truly intrigued him. He was accustomed to the lies of corporate wheeling and dealing, and the glib untruths other women told him in order to get what they wanted from him. Rosy's blunt candour had repeatedly thrown him off-balance, but he realised he liked that about her—he liked the challenge.

'Why rush this?'

'Because I want you to.'

Torn between loving her honesty and hating it, because it demanded too much emotional honesty from him in return, a groan escaped his throat as he lifted her white dress and nudged a thigh between her legs. She gasped when he found her core with his hand beneath her underwear. Clinging to him, she showed him with innocent enthusiasm exactly what she liked. Rosy gave him no chance to seduce her. The problem was holding her back.

'Are you determined to frustrate me?' she demanded at one point, stabbing a passionate glare into his eyes as he lazily stroked her.

'Delay is the servant of pleasure,' he murmured, smiling against her mouth.

'Only if you've got time,' she countered with perfect good sense.

He laughed, loving the fact that she could lighten him to this degree. 'You have an answer for everything,' he scolded with a shake of his head.

'I don't have an answer for you,' she admitted.

Good.

'And I'm done with chaste kisses and teasing caresses,' she added. 'If you don't really want me in your bed, you only have to say and I'll go.'

'I want you,' he growled.

Three words that proved to be the key to the castle where she had kept her technical virginity imprisoned for all these years. The only downside—and it was a big one—was that Xander still sounded so matter-of-fact. She had hoped he might be swept away by passion, as she was. Would it ever be possible—for anyone— to break through his emotional armour? If so, a virgin was surely the least likely candidate.

Suddenly, her confidence disappeared. Drawing up her knees, she buried her face in them, muttering, 'Sorry…'

'Why?' Xander demanded. 'What are you frightened of? Letting go?'

That final moment of trust when she lost control? Yes, maybe. But it was so much more than that; she wanted something more from Xander, and yet she feared he had nothing more to give her.

'Shall I take you back to the party?' he asked.

'Yes, and no.'

Xander gave a confused smile at her reply. She knew

he'd take her back if she asked, but wasn't this new life of hers supposed to be about new experiences?

Rolling onto her back, she turned her head to look at him. Arms folded behind his head, he seemed in no hurry to convince her one way or the other. He was so damn hot. Lifting herself, she moved across his body to drop a kiss on his lips, and then pulled back before he could catch her.

'Have you done this before?'

She wasn't prepared for the shrewd question, and shook her head honestly.

He sighed. 'If you'd told me before I brought you here—'

'I wanted to come with you.'

'You'd be safer going back to the party. You don't belong in my world.' His voice was gravelly.

Stung, she sat up. 'Not good enough for you?'

'Not experienced enough to really know what you're doing. You're too good for me, if you must know.' There was a long pause. 'So you're a virgin?'

'Technically? No.'

'Technically?' Xander repeated, bewildered. 'What's that supposed to mean?' He reached out and brushed a few strands of hair back from her brow, as though he had to touch her in some way.

'It means I've never had penetrative sex with a man but I've done...other things.'

'I love your bluntness.'

'Good, because that's all you'll get from me.'

'But you should have told me.'

'When? Should I have made an announcement at the Panigiri?'

Xander's mouth tugged at one corner. 'It is rather unusual to be a virgin at your age. Unless...' His expression darkened. 'I've had a feeling ever since I met you that something rather nasty happened to you at some point. What happened?' Then he sat up suddenly. 'My brother didn't—'

'Achilles? No.' Placing her forefinger over Xander's mouth to give her a chance to explain, she said, 'Alexa saved me from him in time.

'I swear to you Achilles didn't hurt me. Alexa didn't give him chance. I'm fortunate enough to be able to say that I've never been subjected to a brutal attack. My inexperience when it comes to men is purely down to lack of opportunity, because I always put my education first.'

'Thank you for your honesty, but Achilles should never have put you through that ordeal. Whether he succeeded or not is immaterial. No woman should be bullied mentally or physically, let alone subjected to brute force.' Grim-faced, Xander shook his head as he added, 'That man has so much to answer for. And, as for you...' His expression changed, softened, as he brought her into his arms. 'I stand by my statement: you don't belong in my world.'

'How do you know where I belong?' Indignation spiked inside her as she pulled away from him and sat up. Xander sat up too, and was all coiled energy. 'And what is *your* world, anyway?' she flared. 'Is it on the streets—or in the boardroom? Or living the high life, escorting a revolving door of supermodels? Do you even know?' She hated bringing up his past, but they had to get this straight. 'You don't have the faintest idea what I want.'

'Where's the prim little teacher now?' he mocked, but she could see she'd disconcerted him.

'Are you the only one who's allowed to decide on my behalf then? Don't patronise me, Xander. Why did you even bring me here? Was it to seduce the *prim little schoolteacher* just because you were bored?'

'You,' he observed admiringly, 'are an extremely provocative woman—'

Why that proved to light the blue touchpaper to her white-hot desire, she had no idea. Whether she moved first or Xander did really didn't matter. He drove his mouth down on hers while she grabbed his shoulders and tangled their limbs together. Pressing close enough to feel every fibre of his being against hers stirred Rosy's hunger into a raging fire.

As Xander rolled his hips against her most sensitive core, mimicking the act she longed for, she claimed a greedy release through the thin material of her dress that hit her long and hard. When she removed the rest of her clothes and ripped open his shirt she gasped with ecstasy to feel warm naked flesh on flesh. Touch and instinct led her inexperienced hands to trace his savage beauty, while Xander's skilful fingers had already taken her to the brink of the abyss again. And this time he did something new. Spreading her thighs, he made her watch as he sent her flying, transforming extreme pleasure into a surge of wicked release. The starburst of sensation was so powerful it rattled her soul. He made her feel so safe she wanted more— Which made her shock all the greater when he pulled back, still clearly aroused.

'What did I do wrong?'

'You? Nothing,' he said.

'But what about you? You haven't...'

Xander, having already left the bed, was already getting dressed.

'Me? I'm fine. You're satisfied, aren't you—for now?'

So, there would be more to come—or not? She couldn't tell from his face. She wasn't his type, she knew that—or maybe her inexperience had put him off? Which was it?

She'd probably get no more answers tonight. Following him out of the bed, she smoothed her hand down the precious dress before putting it on again and shrugging into the little jacket. There was no graceful way to do this—or to locate her missing glasses, which she remembered Xander taking off downstairs. Had he put them down in here? She patted around for them, trying to keep out of Xander's way while he looked party-ready almost at once. How gauche she must appear to him.

'We should be getting back,' he prompted when she finally found her glasses and put them on.

'Yes—' She almost ran to the door, feeling as if she'd made a complete and utter fool of herself.

'Hey—wait up,' Xander called out, but only to return the gold-coin necklace.

'Thanks.' She plucked it from his hand, and returned to the party with her head held high, still questioning why a man like Xander Tsakis could want her as he so obviously had, and could give her pleasure beyond imagining, only to pull away at the very last minute.

Curses fired off in his head as he headed back to the celebration with Rosy, who was quite obviously bewildered and upset by his behaviour. She'd put the crown of flowers back on her head, but it was perched rather precariously at a tilt. Could he touch her to correct it without wanting her? After what had just happened, he doubted it.

He'd pulled back to save her from further hurt. She was not his usual type of woman, and didn't understand the rules he played by. Rosy's decision to have sex with him would represent more of a commitment on her part than he wanted or needed. He had pleasured her because something inside him needed to bring her that release. To watch her, to hear her, and to kiss away her incredulous tears when it had all got too much for her, was the only proof he'd needed that it would never be possible to have sex with Rosy and then just forget her and walk away. He'd thought that pulling back had been the right thing to do. Rosy was too valuable an asset for the island, one that Praxos could not afford to lose because of him.

'Let me fix this—'

'What?' She backed away as he reached out and then realised he was trying to adjust her crown.

'Before it hits the floor,' he explained. 'Perfect,' he added, standing back to admire his handiwork.

'I've never been a queen before. But even queens have to work, so please excuse me—'

And with that she was gone, heading back to the party at warp speed.

He sensed that Rosy was hurt and humiliated, which was the very last thing he had intended. But he couldn't offer anything permanent, which was what she deserved. She was not the type to take to bed lightly and deserved a regular guy with a regular job, who would cherish her. Praxos could not afford to lose Rosy, certainly not through some misstep of his, so it was vital that he made her see that the reason things had to be on his terms was to protect her feelings, and to stop Rosy expecting too much of him.

The sound of crashing plates distracted him and drew him to the dance floor, where he found Rosy and Alexa adding more plates to the stack destined to end up in pieces on the floor.

'Now we banish evil for another year,' Alexa announced with satisfaction.

'Ya-Ya!' Using the affectionate term for a Greek grandmother, he made sure Alexa had her fair share of plates and gestured for the other revellers to make space so she could join them.

'That was nice of you,' Rosy remarked coolly when he returned to her side.

Not really. He'd wanted the chance to have Rosy to himself. Major fail in that department, he concluded wryly as she pushed a pile of plates into his hands. Balancing the plates in one hand, he took hold of Rosy's hand with his other to lead her onto the dance floor, with the instruction, 'Smash them.' He handed her half the stack. 'You know you want to.'

The silent message she fired into his eyes didn't have much to do with smashing plates on the floor, and everything to do with smashing them over his head. He winced internally but knew he deserved her silent condemnation. They ended up competing for the loudest crash, and finally she was relaxed and laughing by the time the last plate hit the floor.

The band began to play music for the *kalamatiano*, the traditional dance of Greece. Taking Rosy with him, he joined the line of dancers, allowing the earthy rhythm to propel them back and forth. When Rosy tightened her hand around his and looked into his eyes, he gave an inward sigh of relief. Seemed the magic of the old ritual hadn't died.

'No one will notice if we leave,' she murmured invitingly when the band fell silent. 'And don't you dare ask me if I'm sure about this.'

CHAPTER EIGHT

MAYBE SHE SHOULD have more sense, but where was the fun in that? She'd thought last time that if they only had one night it would be the best night of her life. That hadn't changed. Xander's eyes promised more pleasure, and that was all Rosy's recently awakened body cared about. She'd already lost control in his arms more than once. What part of *I want this* was there left for him to fight? She was going into it with her eyes wide open. Xander didn't offer love, so it was up to Rosy to protect her heart.

'Would you like to swim first?' he suggested as they crossed the beach on their way to the Big House.

'Oh, yes...' Wild, free, the cooling wash of the sea would maybe calm her down a little—she needed something.

Slipping off her sandals, she ran ahead to leap into the surf. Lifting her arms, she turned full circle, paying homage to the moon, and to her amazing life on Praxos. Then she realised that Xander was watching her, his expression masked by the shadows.

She called out to him, 'Is it safe to swim here at night?'

'With me, yes,' he confirmed.

As he drew close, she saw that Xander had stripped down to his boxers, which was her cue to take off the beautiful dress and bolero jacket once again. He'd already seen her naked body and had found it easy to pull away, so she was sure he'd cope with the sight of her in her underwear. Folding her clothes, she left them safe on a flat rock, where they couldn't be touched by the waves.

'Are you going to take this off too?' Xander asked, his tone husky and low.

Now she remembered the crown of flowers, which he was carefully removing. Dragging deep on his familiar scent, she allowed the warmth of his body to infuse her with confidence. A cold shower was said to cool ardour. The sea should be equally effective, and she could do with something to put on the brakes. Rosy's heart and body ruled her completely when she was with Xander. Her clear-thinking mind didn't stand a chance.

'Are you a confident swimmer?' he asked before they set off. 'If not, paddle along the shoreline.'

'I'm confident,' she stated firmly.

This late in the year the water was tepid, having had the burning summer sun to warm it up. Wading through the shallows, she sank with relief into deeper water and began to swim. Under the moon, beneath the stars, living the dream, the silence was complete.

'You swim well,' Xander observed. 'Can you see that small fast craft?' he asked as they swam further out to sea. 'Make for that.'

Treading water, she looked around and soon spotted the sleek red speedboat he was referring to.

Xander was completely at home in the water. His

bronzed skin gleamed wetly in the moonlight, while his hard-muscled shoulders offered a tempting harbour. But she could look after herself. And would have to, Rosy concluded determinedly.

'Shall we take it out?' he suggested as they drew alongside the impressive red craft.

'Won't the owner mind?'

'Shall I ask him?'

'Ah.' Lightbulb moment. 'This is your boat.'

Xander's muscles flexed as he pulled himself on board. 'Give me your hand,' he said as he reached over the side to haul her up. 'Are you cold?'

'A little,' she admitted.

Opening a hatch, he retrieved a thick, rough blanket, which he tossed around her shoulders. How beautiful he was…such a primal force. Save for this million-dollar boy-toy, he could have been a local roustabout from the docks. And he was all the more attractive for that.

'We could swim back to shore, if you prefer?' he offered.

'If you don't take me for a fast, hard ride right now, I'll never get over it.'

His lips pressed down in a wry smile. 'You asked for it. Strap in.' Xander angled his stubble-blackened chin towards a seat that looked as if it belonged in a Formula One racing car. 'This is the most beautiful shoreline in the Mediterranean, and if you haven't seen it by moonlight, then you should…'

There was nothing about this night she would change, Rosy decided as Xander eased the throttle forward and they took off with a roar, but as the mighty needlepoint prow of the powerboat lifted and the wind snatched at her hair she longed for that part of Xander that he didn't show to the world to last beyond tonight. At least here on the sea, stripped-back to a raw individual, he could show his love of nature as well as his love for Praxos, and with a passion she found infectious. Maybe it was only here that Xander could be truly free.

Anyway, there was no point in wishing for the moon when it was so far out of reach, but for this one night when she wanted to believe that anything was possible. Her body wholeheartedly agreed and yearned for more, for everything, as she glanced towards Xander, standing like a titan at the controls of his powerful boat.

He dropped anchor and they swam back to shore. Wading out of the surf side by side, Rosy felt as if they'd drawn closer, though it had been impossible to say very much above the scream of the engine and the rush of the wind. Just being together felt good, and she believed that she had come to know Xander a little better, thanks to everything that had happened—good and bad—tonight.

The beach was deserted and Xander was keen to head off, but Rosy couldn't find her shoes. 'I have the dress and jacket, but not the shoes.' And with the moon hiding behind a cloud, it was too dark to find anything… but each other. Linking fingers, they pressed hungrily against each other and Xander solved the shoe problem by swinging her into his arms. She felt so safe nestled against him as he strode up the path to the Tsakis family home.

The house was silent and empty. Lowering her to her

feet, Xander cupped her face and kissed her, tenderly at first, and then with increasing passion. There was no chance to talk, none needed. In the morning everything would be back to normal, but for this one night she would live the dream. A dream of her own making, Rosy determined when Xander steadied her on her feet outside his bedroom door. Taking hold of his hand, she led him into the room.

They took a shower first, to get rid of the saltwater. Or at least that was the original intention. It all went crazy back to front when Xander turned on the shower before they undressed and backed her up against the wall beneath the spray. He silenced her laughing screams of protest with a kiss, and as she wrangled with his belt buckle Xander skilfully removed what few scraps of damp clothing she was still wearing.

Faced by the tough, tanned body of a gladiator and Xander's darkly glittering glamour, she accepted happily that there'd be no going back now. There wasn't an inch of Xander's powerful frame that wasn't designed for pleasure. And there was more than enough room to make love in his vast black marble shower.

The shock of his firm warm skin on her softer yielding frame was almost enough to tip her over the edge, and when his large hands began to map her breasts…

'I can't hold on!'

'Did I ask you to?'

That was all the encouragement she needed, and Xander's knowing hands made sure she enjoyed each powerful wave of pleasure until they finally subsided and she was ready for more. 'I think you enjoyed that,' he commented in a lazy drawl.

That could not begin to describe the sensation still streaming through her. Standing on tiptoe, she wound her arms around his neck, exposing her breasts and anything else he wanted to touch. Her nipples peaked, demanding his attention, while every other erotic zone she possessed pulsed with need. Throwing back her head to grab some much-needed air, she whimpered softly at the lightest brush of Xander's sharp black stubble on her neck, and when he cupped her naked buttocks she cried out with excitement to feel the proof of how much he wanted this too—so much, his formidable erection thrusting and straining in anticipation of reaching its home.

Dipping at the knees, he nudged and brushed the hungriest part of her with his mouth. This was more than sex. This was what being wanted felt like, if only for tonight. Touching and teasing as warm water cascaded over them in an endless stream, Xander proved how expert he was at all of this, and he soon had her teetering on the edge again.

'Let go,' he encouraged in a husky tone.

She hadn't even realised how easy it would be to obey him, and she threw herself over the edge into pleasure with a shriek of, *'Yes!'*

'Not here,' he instructed when she greedily rubbed herself against him in search of more. If she'd had even half her wits about her she would have realised that he was saying that in a calm, controlled tone. But she was too far gone for caution, and could only think of the pleasure still in store.

Her voice sounded hoarse, the words urgent, when she demanded, 'Where, then?'

'Bed,' Xander said simply as he switched off the shower.

Final decision time. Was sex without emotion enough for her? It would have to be, because that was all she would get from Xander. And she wanted him—or the pretence of having all of him, at least, for this one special night. Not a chance she was turning back now.

The fierceness in Rosy's expression convinced him that, even though she was inexperienced, he was right in thinking they could have this one night and then part without regrets. They understood. They knew. They accepted. A woman as special as Rosy could dictate terms even he was prepared to accept. He'd fought long enough against his hunger for Rosy, a woman who refused to play by the rules. Holding back had never been a consideration before, but Rosy was worth the wait. He chose his partners carefully, making sure they were always on the same page as him, wanting sex without consequences, repercussions or regret. They could ask him for anything, but not love or long-term commitment, because he would always move on.

Rosy deserved better, but for this one night she had made it clear that she wanted him to be the perfect lover, because that was what she needed. Tomorrow was another day, when they would both move on. And not with some lavish gift from him, because that would mean nothing to Rosy. All she cared about was Praxos and her beloved school, so she'd have his pledge of friendship and support going forward.

She almost broke him when he laid her down on
the bed, by touching his face with a cherishing hand.
Open feelings were a rare honour between them. He
had come to believe Rosy was as locked-up emotionally as he. Avoiding emotional entanglement had been
drummed into him as a child, while Rosy had learned
that lesson later but it was by no means diminished by
a shorter passage of time.

The women in the brothel where his mother had lived
and died had been kind enough to the orphan child, but
had their own set of problems, which meant they were
always forced to abandon him in the end. Eleni and
Romanos had showered him with love, but even that
hadn't been enough to fully heal his scars. Avoiding
that pain had become his life's work, but for this one
night he would think only of Rosy.

Was this what love felt like? She had never felt so warm
in her heart, or so safe in every way. Yet Xander blazed
with restless energy. Experience radiated from him like
sparks from a Catherine wheel. There was always the
possibility she would disappoint him in bed. She was
hardly a practised siren. And another problem—what
would happen when the passion she'd guarded for so
long was unleashed? She'd already experienced a noisy
warm-up which only hinted at what might yet be to
come. But he was so careful with her she was able to
calm down enough to convince herself that if this was
just one short chapter in the book of her life she'd read
it with relish and then move on.

She'd made big decisions before. Leaving everything
she knew to come and live on Praxos had worked out

well for her. Was this really so different? *Yes!* Inner
warnings aside, if she took what was offered and didn't
expect anything more from him, she'd be fine. Fine-
ish. Maybe not fine at all, but she wanted this illusion
of closeness with Xander so much. When he loomed
over her and she felt his power bind with hers, it was as
if they were two people coming together because they
couldn't stay apart.

'You're beautiful,' he said as he peeled away the
towel she was wrapped in. 'Like a precious volume,
full of stories waiting to be told—'

'Well, you suddenly turned into a romantic,' she exclaimed softly with surprise.

'Only with you,' Xander confessed gruffly as he
teased every part of her with kisses.

Being close to him like this allowed her to feel the
loneliness Xander carried deep inside him. She could
only guess at the secrets of a man who confided in no
one, but she had some clues in his love of nature and this
island. Whatever the world thought of Xander Tsakis,
driven billionaire, this man was sensitive beneath his
steely armour.

'Make love to me,' she whispered, staring up into
his eyes.

Taking hold of her hands, he rested them on the pillows above her head and then he traced a line of fire
along her throat with his kisses.

Expecting Xander to fill the empty space in her heart
was a wish too far. Asking him for sex was much more
realistic. He made her feel beautiful and, with his calm
control, he made her relax enough to believe she could
be desirable, at least for this one night.

As he released her hands she laced her fingers through his hair, allowing the thick black whorls to spring against her hand. She might be inexperienced, but she didn't need a textbook for this; her body took the lead, and nature did the rest. Arching her spine, she thrust her breasts towards him in open invitation, and with only one word on her lips. 'Please…'

'I've always found good manners irresistible,' Xander teased with a sexy grin.

While she was left floating weightless in his erotic net, he kissed and aroused every part of her until she was composed entirely of sensation. When he cupped her buttocks, lifting and tilting her to his preference, she knew she couldn't hold on.

'Not yet,' he murmured as he swiftly protected them both. 'I'll tell you when.'

Rosy doubted she could wait.

'You must wait,' Xander ordered as if he could read her mind.

His tone was so measured and firm she found it possible to follow his instruction until finally, in one glorious moment, he urged, 'Now—!' And took her deep.

Accepting the command with greedy relief, she screamed out her pleasure as the most intense release yet consumed every part of her. How he stretched her—filled her, making sensation an all-encompassing thing. But what mattered more to Rosy was that at last, both emotionally and physically, they were one.

Fingers clamped around his buttocks like vices of steel to keep him in place meant she could buck furiously in response to his every thrust. Did he have any idea how much she needed this? How could he, when even she had not known?

'Greedy,' he murmured with satisfaction when eventually she quietened.

'Do you blame me?'

Their eyes met and held for the longest time, until Rosy fell back, replete, on the pillows.

CHAPTER NINE

HE HAD NOT spent his entire life governing his emotions only to give vent to them now, but he ached to do so. Only Rosy made him feel like this—exposed, even vulnerable, with feelings so powerful they refused to be subdued.

'What do you want?' he asked himself, not realising he was speaking his thoughts out loud.

Rosy thought he was talking to her. 'You—*this*,' she said with absolute conviction.

Sex would eclipse everything, saving them both from emotional involvement. He was a master in the art. If pleasure were the only goal, he could deliver that, no problem. Moving her hand away when she reached for him again, he warned, 'Not yet. It's time to learn about the benefits of control.'

'Control is everything to you,' Rosy complained, making the mantra he lived by seem more like a curse.

'The reward will be worth the wait,' he promised with a smile against her mouth.

'Spare me the clichés,' she exclaimed, jerking back. 'I am not an object, or a well-trodden path. I am an individual with unique needs and passions, and I refuse to be tortured by you.'

'Oh, do you?' Coming hot on the heels of the most fabulous sex he'd ever had, that made him laugh out loud. He'd never seen sex as also being fun before, but Rosy changed everything she touched into something rare and precious. It was that freedom she gave him that made him laugh. Unfortunately, his laughter only made her angry.

'Will you never take me seriously?' she demanded with a frown.

'Of course I will,' he promised as he tumbled her beneath him.

'But you're still laughing at me,' she said, pouting adorably.

'Not laughing at you—laughing with you. You make me happy.'

'I do?' She frowned again, but this time she seemed amazed.

Not half as much as he was, but this was a very special woman, whose innate honesty had lifted the high bar he'd always set to a level he doubted any other woman could come close to.

'You are an impossible brute,' she raged, refusing to join him in laughter. 'I don't know why I don't—'

'What?' he soothed, bringing her into his arms.

'You can't expect me to laugh along and respond emotionally just as you'd like on those rare occasions when you decide to show me a part of yourself.'

It was his turn to frown down at Rosy. 'What more do you want of me?'

'That you don't remain as cold as a machine for most of the time, only coming to life when we make love.'

'Is this cold? Is this machine-like?'

She gasped with pleasure as he gave her a little of what she liked, but then complained, 'Now you're taking advantage of me, when I just want you to feel the same as I do—'

'Which is?' he asked with genuine interest.

'That this is intimate and ours alone, and that tonight is something we'll both remember for ever.'

'What makes you think I won't remember it?'

'I never know with you,' Rosy admitted with her usual honesty. 'Sometimes you're like quicksilver, changing so fast that just when I think I'm getting to know you I realise that I don't know you at all. And you don't play fair,' she complained as his hands began to rove enticingly.

'I don't remember promising to play fair...'

It wasn't long before Rosy lost control again—he made sure of it, but when she came to this time her mood had changed. 'You'll distance yourself after tonight,' she predicted grimly, as if second sight had not been granted to him alone. 'I might as well invest in a sex toy now—'

'A *what*?' he exclaimed. 'Is that all I am to you?' He was surprised by how much that hurt.

'Maybe,' she said, rolling away. 'It feels like that's all I mean to you.'

'No!'

Almost before the protest—one he'd made so many times before—had left his lips, Rosy went in for the kill. 'We both know I'm nowhere near as experienced as you, but I still believe there should be more to sex than sensation.'

'There is,' he said fiercely. 'Do you think I feel nothing?' They'd experienced it all, hadn't they? He had. And he felt stung by her remark. What he'd shared with Rosy was unlike anything he'd ever known before. There had been nothing usual, let alone machine-like, about it. She'd stripped his emotions bare.

Looking at him straight in the eyes, she seemed to judge him in her own way. Several long moments passed and then she whispered, 'Kiss me.'

When he embraced her, gently this time, he felt something stir in his heart that he hadn't even known was there.

'Not like that,' she said, laughing as she reached up to grab his shoulders. 'You don't have to treat me as if I'll shatter into tiny pieces. And don't worry about tomorrow, because I won't. Let's just have tonight. And then, if we want nothing more from each other, no harm done.'

Did she mean that? Her words left him feeling strangely empty. Sex without emotion was familiar ground to him, but when the licence for doing that came from Rosy it was surprisingly hard to take.

'Do I have your attention?' she murmured with more than a hint of a naughty smile in her voice.

'One hundred per cent,' he assured her.

'What are you doing now?' she complained when he pulled away from her.

Reaching into his nightstand, he showed her the foil packet.

'Protecting us both again,' she approved as she rested

back on the pillows, watching him put it on. 'Just don't tease me or keep me waiting. I couldn't bear it.'

'I have no intention of doing either,' he promised. 'Are you sure you're ready for more?'

'Are you kidding me?' she whispered, stroking his buttocks until he couldn't resist a moment longer and slid inside her, but this time he did tease her, pulling out completely, only to take her again with one steady, all-consuming thrust. Rosy worked with him as though they'd done this a thousand times, moving rhythmically and fiercely until the immensity of sensation was beyond bearing. This last release eclipsed all the rest, but they didn't stop there. It was as if they would never get enough of each other, and so they continued to make love through the night with a primal energy that consumed them both, as if the barriers they had both erected had finally been breached, unleashing a storm that might take a lifetime to subside.

There were quieter moments when he whispered reassurances in Greek, and laughter at other times that brought them even closer, until finally they lay in silence, each lost in their own thoughts.

This was almost certainly love, Rosy concluded sleepily when she woke the next morning, warmed by a sense of deep contentment. If it wasn't, then what was it? She stretched out an arm to feel for Xander, but his side of the bed was bare. A sliver of light came through the curtains, enough to confirm she was alone. And then she heard the slam of a car door.

Instantly awake, she rocketed out of bed, registering, as she ran to the window, that Xander's side of the bed had been straightened as if he had wanted to conceal the signs of their passionate lovemaking. Fumbling with the heavy curtains, she was in time to see his powerful SUV roar away.

Turning back to face the silence of the room, she felt her stomach plunge at the knowledge that he'd gone to solve that business problem. But he'd left without a word to her. That was how little she meant to him.

She found her beautiful dress, neatly laid out on a chair, together with the rest of her things. Xander must have done that. Surely he'd left a note too...?

No note. No text. No recorded message on her phone.

But that had been their arrangement. She'd always known Xander would keep to his schedule, regardless of what happened between them, and she'd accepted that. She could hardly pretend she didn't know who she was dealing with. Xander Tsakis, beloved by the society gossip pages in countless magazines, had more rumours flying around than he could live up to in several lifetimes. *Lock Up Your Daughters!* had been one ugly headline. And in spite of Xander's countless reassurances, she had to wonder now if that was true. Why should she be any different to the rest?

Humiliation made her cheeks burn red. He hadn't even paused to say goodbye. Yes, they'd both been hungry for sex, and yes, they'd both feasted. But now that was done, it seemed she was done too—Xander was done with her.

For goodness' sake! She was *not* done. She'd been an equal partner in last night. What did she expect from him now—a love letter? *Dear Rosy, thank you for the—*

For the what? Fabulous sex? Accept they'd both had a great time, and get on with your life.

Get on with my life...?

My life is here. And my life is good. Nothing can spoil that.

So why did her heart ache like this? If last night was all they had, she'd take it and move on.

What came next?

Practical matters had always helped to get Rosy through a crisis. So she'd straighten her spine, take a shower...get dressed.

And then? And then she'd get out of here.

He had never felt the loss of a woman before. If it hadn't been for that business emergency he'd already put off once, he would have stayed exactly where he was. As it was, old habits died hard. Knowing he really had to rectify the problem face to face, he'd taken care not to wake a slumbering Rosy, and had taken a shower, dressed and gone straight to the airstrip, where his jet was already fuelled and waiting. Only now they were in the air did he think about leaving a note for her—a text at least. But his team were already seated around the jet's boardroom table, waiting for him to lead the meeting.

There had never been a time when he couldn't move straight on to the next thing, the next task, the next destination, the next woman, without delay or distraction. Rosy had made it clear that she only wanted one night with him. Was it even fair to contact her and raise her hopes? He'd trained his mind to focus and concentrate on whatever was in front of him. But today, this morning, he couldn't get her out of his mind.

Rosy, with her trusting emerald eyes and the smile that curved her lips whenever she countered his sternness with humour. She wasn't even slightly in awe of him, which pleased him, and she didn't want anything from him, unless it was for the school. 'What do you think I could possibly need?' she'd asked in answer to his question one day when he'd walked her back home after yet another Panigiri meeting. 'If *you* feel the need to give more of yourself—tell me more about yourself—I'd love that.' He smiled, remembering the gesture she'd made, arms wide, eyes glowing with candour, as she added, 'But I have everything I need, right here on Praxos.'

It was perhaps that last phrase that reassured him that Rosy would still be there when he returned from dealing with this latest crisis. He just wasn't used to accounting for his whereabouts to anyone else and, from what Rosy had said, she didn't expect him to either. It would all be okay. Part of him said it would be better for Rosy if she never set eyes on him again, while another part urged him to change the rules and hook up with her again. And that part won. It still wouldn't be anything long-term, but if she could make him pause long enough to look around and see the world through Rosy's eyes, that would be enough for him. Appreciating beauty was her gift. It was just a shame she couldn't see how beautiful *she* was, but maybe that was in his gift.

There had to be more to life than fighting fires and signing contracts, he concluded as he disembarked the aircraft. Maybe that was something else he'd have to review. Perhaps he'd send Rosy something after all, to compensate for leaving her before she was awake. It was a problem deciding on a gift, though, because, as she'd said, Rosy already had everything. She was probably the only person on earth who could make him envious. To live with relatively little and yet be truly happy, that was a pearl beyond price in his eyes.

Had he spoiled that for her? He'd never forgive himself if that were the case. He ground his jaw as he settled into the waiting limousine. The thought of Rosy waking and finding him gone and feeling hurt poured molten guilt on top of molten guilt, but it was too late to change things now and anything he said would only sound like an excuse.

Whatever else happened in Rosy's life, he was reassured she'd be okay, because she'd always been okay. She was a survivor, she had resilience and, more than that, she had the one thing he craved above all else, and that was contentment.

CHAPTER TEN

XANDER HAD BEEN gone for what felt like a lifetime, but for what had actually been no more than a matter of a few short months when the call came through. Rosy was walking home across the sand one late afternoon, already missing school on this, the last day of the autumn term. She would have felt better if she'd heard just once from Xander. How was he? Where was he? No one on the island knew, except for his housekeeper, Maria, who wasn't saying. Having reassured Rosy that Xander was okay, Maria's kindly, weather-worn face had become a blank page. Knowing the level of discretion Xander expected from his staff, Rosy hadn't liked to make life awkward for Maria by asking too many questions—

She actually exclaimed out loud when her phone rang.

Could this be him?

Rummaging frantically in her bag, she pulled out her phone, looked at the number and frowned with concern. This was almost more of a shock than hearing from Xander.

'Dad? Are you okay?'

'Rosy...? Is that you?'

The trembling tone of his voice told her things were bad.

'Yes, Dad, it's me. What's happened? What's wrong?'

'I miss you...'

And? He sounded lonely, she registered over the silence on the line. Desperately lonely. So where was Edwina, the woman who had stepped into her father's life when his grief for Rosy's mother was still raw? With the pretence of caring for him, Edwina had taken over the house and his bank account, saying she would save him the worry. Just a short time after that, Edwina had told Rosy that she was no longer welcome in her childhood home.

'Rosy?' her father's voice quavered. 'Are you still there?'

'Yes,' she confirmed. 'Tell me what's happened, and I'll see what I can do.' She tensed as a heart-wrenching sob came over the line.

'I don't know where to begin,' her father admitted brokenly.

'Take a deep breath, and start at the beginning,' Rosy soothed.

'I just need you here, Rosy...to tell me what to do.'

Rosy's heart swelled with love and the need to protect her father. He'd always been weak and easily led, but her mother had loved him all the same. Edwina had promised to look after him, and her father had begged Rosy to give Edwina that chance but, with that hope gone, he did need her and she wouldn't let him down, though a vision of the school flashed into Rosy's mind. She couldn't let the children down either. But term had ended, she reasoned, and although Summer School was about to kick into action, she had drawn up detailed plans to make sure that everything ran smoothly. Alexa and the other helpers would be more than capable of holding the fort until Rosy returned.

'She kicked me out, Rosy.'

Her father's words rang like a klaxon in her head.

'She kicked you out of your own house?'

'I made it over to her. She said it would be easier to deal with the bills, if it was Edwina's name on the deeds.'

I bet she did, Rosy thought. This was worse than she had imagined, but there was no point in crying over spilt milk; she had to put a plan in place to help her father go forward. And for that, she had to be at his side.

What about Xander?

What about Xander?

It was time to abandon the fantasy she'd woven around him, to deal with cold, hard facts. Xander took what he wanted and then walked away. She was nothing special to him. He'd treated her just like another of his many discarded lovers. That hurt like hell, but it also stiffened her resolve to put him out of her mind for good. She'd go to England, sort out her father, then come home to Praxos to start work in the new term. Even a short time away from the island would be a wrench, but she would come back soon enough.

'Where are you now, Dad?' she asked gently. Beneath all his bluff and bluster, she got the feeling that her father was still a frightened little boy.

'I'm at the pub— But I don't know how long I'll be allowed to stay,' he added quickly.

Remembering the big-hearted landlord at their local pub, Rosy knew there was only so much that even the kindest people could take.

'I'll text you as soon as I've booked a flight. Okay?'

Thank goodness she could do that, thanks to Xander paying everyone's back wages, with a hefty bonus on top. But her funds wouldn't last for ever, and it sounded as if her father would need some kind of long-term care solution even if they got his house back for him. He was too vulnerable on his own. Another bridge to face when she came to it, Rosy concluded as she ended the call. Her father wasn't a bad man, he was just a weak man, and she would help him all she could.

Continuing her walk home, Rosy thought about her mother and felt sad. She couldn't even guess the number of hopes and dreams her mother must have sacrificed to devote herself to her father, but wasn't that love in its truest form? Or was love a meeting of equals that required sacrifice and compromise on both sides? There was only one face in her mind at that moment, and a pair of wicked black eyes that could still make her yearn, whether Xander had spared Rosy a passing thought or not.

'*What?* What do you mean, she's gone?' He'd flown home, confident Rosy would be still be there, waiting for him. 'Is she all right?' he asked urgently.

'Fine, as far as I know,' Maria told him in an evasive tone he recognised.

Hadn't he taught her that trick himself?

'This is important, Maria. I have to know where

she's gone.' He stared intently into his housekeeper's eyes. 'Please...'

Maria's internal battle had been written large on her face, but at his final plea she relented. 'Kyria Boom took the ferry to the mainland and, from there, a flight home.'

'Home? Her place is here—' Voice raised, he had to take a moment to collect himself. 'Apologies, Maria, I should not shout at you.' He could not believe how strongly he felt about this. Business should have occupied every portion of his mind while he was away, but Rosy had intruded constantly. All he could think about was suggesting they gorge themselves on each other until their mutual passion blew itself out. Now that option was gone—

Was it?

A hungry smile touched his mouth. He'd follow her and bring her back.

'Why did she leave?'

Maria clearly wasn't comfortable with telling him anything more, and it took her a moment to answer, but finally she said, 'To see her father.'

'Did she leave me a note?'

Maria raised an eloquent eyebrow.

Had he left Rosy a note when he'd left?

No. I had urgent business to attend to that couldn't wait. But I did buy her a gift to say sorry. Isn't that enough?

He palmed the small package in his pocket containing the keys to a serviced apartment in New York, where one of his main business hubs was situated. It was the perfect little love-nest overlooking Central Park.

From there she could help him advance the links he'd made with local schools and plan exchange visits with children from Praxos. Rosy had his father's knack of furthering education. With both her heart *and* her ability, who knew what she could achieve? And they could enjoy each other in total privacy, far away from the curious islanders...

'Can you help her?'

He could see from Maria's face that she was feeling bad for having revealed Rosy's destination.

'It's imperative she comes back,' he stated firmly.

'But don't just send her a message,' Maria pleaded, 'or a messenger to find out how she is.' He was shocked when Maria grabbed hold of his sleeve to show how important she felt this was. 'You're the only one who can bring her home to us.'

The word *home* chimed somewhere deep inside him. He shook it off. He abhorred sentimentality. Rosy had to come back to Praxos because this was where she belonged. The school needed her, Maria missed her, as would all the islanders and, most important of all, Romanos had begged him not to lose Rosy. The suspicion that he himself also needed her, he ignored.

'Thank you, Maria. I appreciate your candour.' Placing a reassuring hand on his loyal servant's arm, he placed a call, instructing his team to fuel up the jet and file a flight plan to London.

The cold hit her the moment she landed. Winter in England was very different to winter in Greece, and with every mile travelled she felt a little sadder. Missing friends and the school she loved was as much as she was prepared to admit right now, because there was no point in missing a man who'd left the bed they'd shared with such passion without a word.

She would return to Praxos as soon as she could, Rosy determined as the cab she'd hired at the airport turned into the heart of the small market town where her father was currently staying. Complete with a picturesque cobbles-paved market square, the half-timbered Tudor buildings seemed frozen in time. They were as quaint as she remembered, but she wasn't here to admire the scenery, but to help her father in any way she could. He might have been bullied into becoming estranged from Rosy, but he was in dire straits, and he needed her.

'Could you drop me off here, please?' The traffic, as always, was snarled up in town, and the Pig and Whistle pub was located in the busiest part of the square.

Paying the cab driver, Rosy hurried across the road. Taking a deep breath outside the gnarled entrance door, she walked into a dimly lit haven of welcoming warmth. Low ceilings and beams added to the sense of a savoury cave, where the appetising smell of roast dinners mingled with the aroma of hops and cold beer. There had always been a happy bustle about the place, and the bar was crowded as usual. She could hear her father's voice above the rest. He'd had a few, she guessed, but at least he sounded in better spirits than the last time she'd spoken to him.

'Dad—' Forging her way through the scrum at the bar, she had almost reached him when a familiar voice called her name.

Xander!

The very last person she had expected to see had

stepped in front of her, blocking her way to the bar. For a moment she was stunned and said nothing, did nothing but lift her chin to stare into Xander's achingly familiar eyes. Anger mingled with surprise—relief too, that he was okay and hadn't disappeared off the face of the earth after all. But above all that was a sense of unreality.

'I don't understand—'

'Not here,' Xander growled in her ear. 'Let your father be for now, while we find somewhere else to talk.'

Mesmerised, she followed him away from the bar. The shock was so great, so sudden, it was as if she couldn't think for herself. Xander was here? Her father was here. Was it possible that Xander had made a trip to the UK just for this? How long had he been in England? Had he flown straight here from wherever he'd been? Was she supposed to believe that he cared enough about her to do that? Her heart jolted, soared then plummeted. She didn't know what to believe. If this was regular care for an employee, it was far more than she had ever expected. If, on the other hand, he was here for more than that reason, why hadn't he contacted her sooner?

Ducking his head to clear a low beam, Xander led the way into a sitting room carpeted with well-worn rugs and old-fashioned brass lamps. 'The landlord said we could use this room,' he explained. 'Come in. We won't be disturbed here.'

He wanted to talk privately? About her father? Or about the night they'd shared? Had Xander ever explained himself—*ever*? No. He issued instructions and others obeyed. Well, not this time. She wanted an explanation. It was the least she deserved.

Her initial fierce reaction was now replaced by so many questions. Had he missed her? Did he ever think about that night? Was she wrong to make so much of it? Wasn't it time to grow up and move on?

Doubts and anger mingled in a lava plume that rose, hot and swift, inside her.

'Why are you here?' she demanded aggressively. 'What do you hope to achieve?'

If Xander was surprised by her antagonistic tone of voice, he didn't react. 'I'm here to help you in any way I can.'

'You'd help me most by not being here,' she admitted bluntly. 'I haven't seen my father for a long time, and so much has changed since we were last together. I need privacy, and the right to tell him I have arrived.'

'Your father's fine, for the moment.'

'For the moment,' she gritted out.

'The landlord is keeping an eye on him for me—'

'For *you*?' she almost exploded, and had to press her lips together to stop herself saying something she'd regret. 'Don't you think he's my responsibility? And, while we're at it, who told you I was here?'

'Maria,' Xander revealed evenly.

His control was beginning to get to her, and she had to remind herself that of course Maria would tell their boss what was going on with Rosy.

'Please sit down,' Xander invited in a tone that held no hint of the lover with whom she'd shared a bed. This was her boss, a man who held her future in the palm of his hand. She didn't want to sit, but she took the seat he indicated. She didn't know what to feel or think. Nothing about this made sense.

Xander's arrival at the simple market town pub, must have hit everyone between the eyes. Even dressed down in jeans, black boots and a soft black cashmere sweater, he was a stunning sight. And yet, in some way, he looked like he belonged here, because Xander had a way of always fitting in. She guessed his early life must have contributed to that. Being able to adapt to any situation had probably saved him. But if he was playing the part of hero today, galloping to the rescue of a maiden in distress, it was time to let him know that she could handle this on her own.

Can I handle him? Can I handle my feelings for Xander?

She had to, Rosy determined, because now she was over the initial shock of seeing him, she had to concentrate on her father and his needs, and keeping her job to pay for those needs.

'So, you dropped everything and flew here,' she probed casually. 'From…?'

'From New York,' Xander supplied. 'Why are you being so defensive, Rosy?'

'Am I?'

Biting her lip to stop herself saying more, she flinched as he continued, 'Shall I get you a soapbox to proclaim to the world: I can do this. I can handle this, without help from anyone?'

He was so close to the truth that her cheeks fired red. Xander had made it sound like another form of vanity. She *could* use his help. Of course she could. Her father had to be her first consideration, and who could do more for him than Xander Tsakis, whose reputation as a caring boss was unrivalled?

'I could use some advice,' she admitted. 'And, potentially, some extra time off,' she added, thinking ahead.

'I'm sure all of that is possible.'

'Do you actually have time to help?' Hurt prompted her outburst, and the words were out before she could stop them.

'I'll make time,' he said firmly.

For this. But not to speak to her before he'd left.

'I need to see my father,' she said, springing up before the hurt could take root and grow stronger.

'Of course—' Xander was at the door ahead of her and, opening it, he stood back.

Her father's face lit up the moment he saw her. 'Rosy! Is that really you? I can't believe it. You're *here*!' He turned to include his friends at the bar. 'This is my daughter, the schoolteacher, home for a visit,' he declared with pride.

And would have come home sooner if her father hadn't begged her to stay away. If only Rosy had ignored him, maybe those dark circles of stress she could see beneath his eyes wouldn't be there.

'Lucky man,' a few of his cronies were commenting, while several more had already turned away, quickly losing interest in the larger-than-life character they had thought they knew when he turned out to be a regular family man. He could be again, Rosy determined fiercely. If she had anything to do with it, her father would be himself as soon as possible.

'Rosy...' Her spine tingled as Xander's voice sounded close behind her. He must have seen this initial scene play out. What did he think of all this? His eyes, as she turned around to face him, were dark and unreadable. 'I'm going to leave you to it,' he said, 'but I have a room here, so—'

How long did he plan to stay?

'Is there anything I can do for you before I go—?'

'You're going?' she blurted.

'Not right away. I'll be here for as long as you need me.'

Would he be away for months like the last time, or did he mean it when he said he'd be there for her? Would she ever understand what made this man tick?

CHAPTER ELEVEN

XANDER HAD ARRANGED a table for two, so that Rosy and her father could reunite over a tasty pub meal. He didn't join them, which Rosy appreciated as she wanted the chance to catch up without distractions, and without her father feeling that he couldn't say too much in front of her boss.

'He's the most remarkable man,' her father enthused as he continued to sing Xander's praises over a gammon steak, crunchy golden potatoes and a fried egg.

But the best was yet to come.

Rosy had to retrieve her dropped jaw from the floor when her father revealed, 'Your boss has arranged for me to attend a private clinic in Switzerland, where I can rest and recuperate from my stressful experiences in clean mountain air.'

'Right…' Rosy was lost for words. She came to, to hear her father add, 'It'll give me a chance to get my head together.'

He said this in such a touchingly hopeful tone she knew she couldn't deny him the chance to take himself out of the ordinary and experience something exciting and new, especially when it could possibly help him.

'That's wonderful,' she agreed. And it was, but shouldn't Xander have discussed this with her first?

Discuss? Was that Xander's way?

Noticing him emerging from the inn's private guest quarters, she decided that now was as good a time as any to confront him about it.

'I'll leave you to enjoy the rest of your meal,' she told her father as she left the table. 'I need to have a word with Xander.'

'Of course,' he said, munching happily.

She didn't hesitate, and launched right in. 'Dad says you've booked him into some clinic in Switzerland. I don't remember discussing this with you.'

Xander's powerful shoulders rose in a casual shrug. 'I have a clinic there—'

What?

'Of course you do,' she commented with a cynical smile.

'You sound surprised. I've owned the Pure Health chain of clinics for some time. I consider this particular facility, high in the Swiss Alps, to be the pearl in that crown. Rest and recuperation is what your father needs. He'll find himself in the most stunning surroundings imaginable. Did I do something wrong?'

Rosy exhaled with frustration as one sweeping ebony brow lifted, making Xander even more attractive, if such a thing were possible, but she had no intention of being swayed by his staggering good looks.

'You should have talked it over with me first.'

'Forgive me.' Hand to chest, he made an attempt to seem contrite and failed miserably. 'Do you ski?'

'Do I what? No. What's that got to do with anything?'

'You can learn,' Xander mused, ignoring her question.

'Maybe, but I don't want to learn—'

'The skiing in Gstaad is excellent at this time of year.'

'If you think I'm coming with you—'

'Of course you're coming with me. Your father will need that reassurance, to help settle him in. Only you can provide that. Don't look so worried,' Xander insisted with a piercing look. 'The therapists at my facility are the best in the world.'

Naturally, she thought.

'I'm sure they are, but you should have warned me what you had in mind.'

'Would you rather your father stayed here, drinking the bar dry with his pals?'

'Of course not, but—'

'I took the action I deemed necessary—with your father's agreement; after all, he is the one in need of help here.'

What could she say to that? Could she risk losing such an amazing opportunity for her father?

'My intention is to remove all stress and worry— for both of you,' Xander explained in a perfectly reasonable tone which, for some crazy reason, drew Rosy's attention to his lips. Memories of the pleasure he could create with that mouth flashed through her brain.

'Well, you've already caused me stress and worry—' True. 'And I don't know anything about this clinic, let alone if it can help my father, as you say it can.'

'The proof of the pudding...' Xander stated with a shrug. 'Don't you think you should give him that chance?'

Rosy glanced at her father. She couldn't leave him here.

'If you think what I've done wrong—?'

'No,' she admitted frustratedly, realising he was out-manoeuvring her. 'It's just the way you go about things.'

Xander's beautiful mouth tugged ruefully at one corner. 'Please forgive me for trying to help you, Rosy. I shall be sure to ask for your permission before I do anything in future.'

'Liar,' she breathed as their stares met and lingered. 'And there's something else,' she added, coming to her senses.

'Hit me,' Xander invited.

'Don't tempt me. This all sounds wonderful to my father, and I can only thank you on his behalf, but it's way beyond my pay grade. And I won't accept charity,' she added firmly, before Xander had chance to speak. 'I'll only agree to this Swiss trip if you allow me to pay back every penny of the cost. I'll need a payment plan, of course—'

'Your coffee's getting cold,' Xander observed, glancing towards the dining table she'd been sharing with her father.

'Are you even listening to me?' Rosy demanded.

'I'm listening,' Xander confirmed with a penetrating stare into her eyes. 'But you should know that the Tsakis family has company schemes in place for staff who need treatment, so you won't have to pay a penny.

All you have to do to help your father recover is to give me your suitcase, and I'll put it in my car.'

'Your limousine's waiting outside?' she guessed, and when Xander shrugged this time she knew there was no point in fighting him all the way to Switzerland, not when this could be the best thing for her father.

'My roll-along is next to the coat stand by the door.'

'Good.'

And with that he was gone, leaving Rosy to urge her father to finish his coffee and come with her.

'It's going to be okay, Dad,' she said, putting her hand over his. 'You've got a wonderful adventure ahead of you, and I'm willing to bet you'll soon be back to your old self.'

'Without your mother?'

'Come on,' she pressed, helping him to his feet. 'Let's go and get your things—'

'You stay—go and talk to your boss; I'll be back in a minute.'

Following her father's stare, she saw Xander on his way to join them.

'Good,' he said. 'I was hoping for a moment to straighten things out between us before we left.'

Rosy's throat dried as she wondered what that meant.

'I wasn't going to say anything,' Xander admitted as they both watched her father go through the door leading to the guest accommodation, 'but I guess I owe you an explanation for the way I left Praxos so abruptly.'

'You guess?'

'All right, I do owe you an explanation.'

The intensity of his stare burned its way through her entire body, touching all her erotic zones along the way.

After all he was prepared to do for her father, she had to at least give him chance to explain.

'This had better be good,' she warned.

'Unexpected news on the business front forced me to leave. My commercial interests fund everything I do.'

'So you left without thinking who you might be hurting?'

He sighed. 'You're obviously not in the mood to forgive me.'

'Forgive you? Is that within my power?'

'I think it should be.'

'I'm sure you do. I should forgive a man who makes love to me as if I'm the only creature on earth he cares about, and who then walks away without a single word of explanation or farewell?'

'I'm sorry, I—'

'Prove it.'

'You are a very hard woman to convince.'

'No. I'm sensible, defensive and wary. Once bitten...'

'I get it,' Xander said quietly as her father reappeared with a small suitcase carrying all the worldly possessions left to him. 'I've hurt you.'

'Yes, you have,' Rosy said truthfully.

'Which means there's only one option open to me,' Xander observed.

She stared into his eyes. 'Which is?'

'I'll have to make it up to you,' he said over his shoulder as he went to carry her father's suitcase to the car.

'Whereabouts in Switzerland are we flying to?' her father asked as the limousine purred away from the kerb.

'Gstaad,' Xander revealed from the front seat, where he was sitting next to the uniformed chauffeur.

'Isn't that rather upscale?' Rosy asked curiously.

Xander's mouth tugged in a smile. 'I call it home.'

'Of course you do,' Rosy said wryly. 'One of your many homes,' she added as the limo hit the high road, remembering a magazine article she'd read.

'Correct,' he confirmed. Xander wasn't ashamed of his success, nor had he any intention of becoming so.

'Better get used to this,' Rosy's father announced, high on bonhomie and the pub's best ale.

Rosy said, 'Tell us about Gstaad; I only know what I've read.'

'It's far more than a prosperous town in the Bernese Oberland—which is a region in the Swiss Alps,' he explained to her father. 'It's a last paradise in an increasingly crazy world.'

'And very glamorous, from what I've heard,' Rosy added, sounding a little apprehensive, he thought.

'It sparkles,' he agreed, thinking Rosy would fit right in. She'd stand out for all the right reasons with her sensitivity to other people's feelings, her straightforward manner and her beautiful, understated appearance. He might have to get rid of those rather ugly glasses, though.

'Gstaad is extremely glamorous,' he confirmed on the heels of that thought. There was no point in pretending otherwise.

'And there's skiing,' Rosy was telling her father, eager to change the subject, he suspected.

'You won't make me ski to the clinic, will you?' her father asked him with alarm.

'You will be transported with the greatest care in a comfortable vehicle,' he promised, eager to reassure the troubled older man.

Settling back for the short drive to the airstrip where his private jet was waiting, he told himself all would be well.

Gstaad, playground of the rich and famous, say hello to your least glamorous guest...

Was this why Xander had fled at top speed after their night of passion? Staring at herself in the full-length cheval mirror in her super-sumptuous suite, Rosy guessed it could be. She'd better hope there was a chance to nip out for a quick shopping trip—if there was anything she could afford in the Swiss town's answer to Shangri-la. She'd just finished breakfast in her room next to her father's, who had rung to say he was running late. Rosy suspected this meant that her father felt as she did, that he didn't have suitable clothes for such a swanky hotel.

Xander clearly hadn't thought this through, she concluded as she stared out of the window at what could have been a Christmas card view. Neither of them had clothes warm enough for a trip to Xander's private clinic, which was located at an even higher altitude he'd told them. However beautiful it looked outside, it would be freezing and icy. Their clothes had been chosen to suit an unsophisticated market town where snowfall was minimal. Plus, homely described her dress sense at the best of times. Or careless, if you didn't feel kind. Her father had barely had the chance to rescue anything before being booted out of his home. And where was

Xander when she needed him? Had he left already for his next glamorous destination?

More likely, he was warmly settled into his fabulous ski-in, ski-out eyrie, high up in the mountains, far away from her little problems, like where to buy cheap, warm knickers?

There was nothing cheap about Xander. He was all private jet and super-car transport, and had probably forgotten what a shop looked like. With a puff of frustration she picked up the phone, but before the line had chance to connect a discreet knock sounded on the door.

Xander? No. His knock would be imperative, not discreet.

She was right. A smiling housekeeper greeted her, before standing aside to allow a team of porters laden with goods to parade into Rosy's room. There was even a gown rail with hanging clothes.

'On the instruction of Herr Tsakis,' the immaculately uniformed housekeeper explained. 'And we have more clothes for your father,' she reassured Rosy, who must have been standing there, mouth open, looking even more foolish than she felt.

Could she accept all this?

High-flying principles quickly took a dive in the face of so much tempting fashion. She'd never been able to afford very much, and this was excess piled on excess. Plus, someone, probably Peter, had taken a lot of trouble to arrange this for her, so it would be rude not to at least take a look...

'You have some lovely warm things here,' the housekeeper approved, with a glance out of the window before she left.

There was so much to sort through. The most amazing lingerie for starters… Had that arrived by mistake? As Rosy held the delicate flimsies against her body, the thought crossed her mind that this could be Xander's invoice, giving her a way to pay him back. It had better not be!

Calm down…

He didn't want her; he'd walked out with nary a backward glance, remember that. He'd almost certainly had nothing to do with the actual choice of clothes. They'd been purchased on his behalf. And, obviously, whoever had chosen them had taken care to cover every angle… She laughed and her mood changed for the better as she held up a thong composed of translucent gauzy fabric that was clearly the product of a sleepy solitary silkworm working late on a Friday night.

Just so long as she didn't fall down that slippery slope to fantasy land again. And she still had plenty of clean underwear in her case—good, sturdy, sensible stuff.

What fun was that?

Okay, so she'd wear the flimsies under thermal leggings and a long-sleeved top. Job done.

This was like being in a movie, Rosy decided as she viewed herself, togged up in her brand-new clothes. There was no denying that the stylish ski-wear suited her. It was just a shame about the fraud underneath. The sleek form-fitting jacket with its hood fringed in the softest fake fur, teamed with slim-fitting pants, belonged on an Olympic skier rather than a teacher, more accustomed to Greek sunshine than sliding down a mountain on her backside.

CHAPTER TWELVE

ROSY WAS STILL in a bubble of concentration when another knock sounded on the door. *Xander?* No. The housekeeper with yet another parcel. 'Your new spectacles,' she explained. 'You must wear sunglasses at all times outside, to avoid snow-blindness. Each pair has your prescription lenses in place, so you will be able to see the beauty surrounding you quite clearly.'

Just where she was going would be enough—though with Xander at the steering wheel, nothing was certain. And how on earth did anyone know the prescription for her glasses?

'Herr Tsakis arranged it,' the housekeeper revealed, before Rosy had a chance to ask the question.

Of course. Xander knew everything. About everyone. Except when it came to Rosy's heart. But he had been thoughtful, she conceded, in a strictly employer/employee sort of way. And the sunglasses were amazing. She'd never owned anything quite so glamorous before. No tape, no cracks, nothing to scratch her nose—just sheer designer deliciousness.

She stared at her reflection with bemusement, and was still staring when another knock came on the door.

Her heart pounded a tattoo, but this time her father walked in. And he looked amazing. She could hardly take in the transformation. The heavy tailored jacket suited him, as did the alpine hat with its cheeky feather. He looked like a vintage film star, strutting his stuff in a place he was thoroughly accustomed to, rather than a mixed-up English gentleman struggling to know where he belonged.

'Dad!' She hurried to give him the biggest hug ever. 'You look amazing!'

'As do you,' he exclaimed. 'Someone around here has excellent taste.'

'Xander's PA,' she said quickly, not wanting her father to get any ideas about his daughter and their friend the billionaire.

'Xander's downstairs,' he said, adding without pausing for breath, 'Come on, Rosy, we can't keep him waiting for us—'

Just like the film star she'd thought him, her father offered his arm.

Why hadn't Xander let her know he was downstairs? Why tell her father but leave Rosy out of the loop? Because her father was the reason they were here, sensible Rosy—the one who wasn't befuddled by Xander—reminded her.

Her heart nearly stopped altogether when she caught sight of Xander waiting in the lobby. Wearing an all-black outfit, and at least a head taller than any other man present, he was definitely the centre of attention.

'Speed up, Rosy,' her father insisted, tugging at her arm.

Xander was polite but cool—much warmer towards

her father than Rosy. He kept up the required amount of polite conversation on the drive to the clinic. Could he sense that now the moment had arrived both Rosy and her father felt nervous, not knowing what to expect?

They needn't have worried, as they soon discovered that Xander's clinic was a beautiful, light-filled sanctuary where everyone they met seemed gentle and kind.

'I can never thank you enough for this,' Rosy told Xander as they stood together while her father disappeared through swing doors, to be introduced to his new home for the next few weeks. Knowing he would be well looked after, and have the opportunity to rest and recuperate in such a purposeful, well-organised place, seemed nothing short of a miracle.

'Your father has expressed a wish to try both skiing and sky-diving,' he informed her as he led the way to the car.

'Hopefully not both at the same time,' Rosy observed dryly as she climbed into the SUV.

'What would you like to do for the rest of the day?' Xander asked as he slipped a pair of sunglasses on to protect his eyes against the snow.

Ruling out several very bad ideas currently crowding into her mind, all of which involved Xander in a state of undress, she said sensibly, 'I'd like the chance to take everything in, and then rest before I see my father tomorrow.'

'Ah…'

'Ah?' she repeated with concern.

'The doctors have recommended two or three weeks of uninterrupted therapy, which means no visits.'

'They spoke to you about that, and not me?' she

said with affront. 'But what if he needs me? What if he doesn't like it at the clinic? He won't thrive in unfamiliar surroundings without a regular visit from someone he knows. I can't just abandon him and go home.'

'Who's saying you're going anywhere?'

'So I'm your captive now?'

'You're my guest,' Xander informed her.

'At the hotel? I can't afford to stay there for several weeks.'

'Let me reassure you that the hotel is also part of the staff package.'

She huffed disbelievingly. 'I'm expected to believe that you house all your staff in Gstaad's most prestigious hotel?'

'Believe what you like. I wouldn't house my staff anywhere that I myself wouldn't choose to stay.'

If she'd thought for one moment that Xander was drowning her in luxury for any ulterior motive he'd just made it clear that she'd be wrong. She was one of many employees he was looking out for. Nothing more!

Late-night fantasies apart, if it weren't for her father, she wouldn't be here. Who needed their heart trampling on a regular basis? She firmed her jaw but couldn't resist glancing at Xander. In profile, he looked as resolute as she felt.

'Can he keep his phone, at least?' she asked with concern.

'I believe he'll be discouraged from making contact with the outside world, but there are no strict rules about phones at the clinic. If he feels the need to call you he can, but my advice is that you don't contact him. Just give him the chance to find himself again.'

'Do you think that's possible?'

'I believe anything's possible,' Xander stated coolly.

Even you finding your heart? Rosy wondered, feeling yet again that Xander had all his emotional barriers very firmly in place.

'We'll park here, and go up in the gondola—'

'Up where?' she asked, glancing around.

'Up the mountain.' Tipping his dark glasses down his nose, Xander looked at her with amusement.

Rosy was not amused. The gondola station appeared to be a hive of activity, with skiers and snowboarders cramming onto lifts and into small, enclosed bubbles that swept perilously up the mountain in a never-ending stream.

'Up there?' she murmured dubiously, craning her neck.

'Unless you'd prefer to grab some climbing gear and go on foot?'

She shot him a glance. 'What will we do when we get *up* there?'

'Oh, I don't know.' Xander's lips pressed down as he pretended to think about this. 'Ski, maybe?' he said as he came around to her side of the vehicle to help her out.

'But I don't ski... Oh, I get it. This is you teasing me.'

'Would I?'

The expression on his face was so darkly attractive Rosy's entire body urged her to go along with whatever Xander had planned.

'Yes, I think you would,' she stated, feeling a curl of excitement growing.

'If you won't ski, I'll send you down on a tea tray,' he threatened.

'Not funny.'

Xander's mouth quirked as he went to the back of the vehicle, emerging moments later with ski boots and a pair of skis. Putting the boots on, he turned to her. 'Ready?'

'For anything,' Rosy murmured dryly. 'But won't I need boots too?'

'You don't ski,' Xander observed with perfect good sense. 'So, are you coming or not?'

She guessed he would park her in a café while he skied. She could hardly complain, after what he'd done for her father.

With some apprehension, she allowed him to usher her into one of the gondolas. It didn't stop on its round trip up the mountain, which was terrifying. Skiers and snowboarders got out, swung their lethal weapons, in the form of skis and snowboards, within inches of her head and then Xander ushered her into the moving pod. The doors slid to, and they were enclosed in their own private bubble.

Leaning back against the window, Xander surveyed her with a brooding stare. What was he thinking… What? Her body had plenty of ideas, while Rosy contented herself with imagining Xander ripping blue murder out of the piste, though she doubted he could look any sexier than he did now. And then their bubble cleared the base station and began to rise into the vastness of the mountains above.

Xander blamed the gondola's swinging action at the start of the ascent that threw Rosy into his arms. Never one to ignore an opportunity, he closed his arms around her. What happened next was…mutual lust? It was certainly something. Rosy's hands were everywhere, finding him through the thickness of his ski pants. He groaned as she exclaimed in triumph. Using both hands, she measured both his length and his girth, and with a sound of satisfaction she pressed herself hungrily against him. There was enough heavy breathing to steam up the gondola. What had happened to his much-vaunted control? Lost baggage, maybe.

Theé mou!

How could he have forgotten how perfect Rosy felt in his arms? But then, quite suddenly, she thrust her fists against his chest and turned away, as if her trembling body was at odds with her sensible mind. He pulled back immediately. It wasn't often he misread a situation. In fact, it had never happened before. And it wasn't happening this time, he registered as Rosy grabbed him back again.

'Don't do this. I want you,' he growled.

Rosy was on fire. 'I want you too,' she insisted fiercely.

'But you pulled away.'

'I'm allowed a moment of sensible thought, aren't I?'

'And what did your sensible self tell you?'

'Live for the moment.' Her eyes darkened as they stared into his. 'No more talking—'

Past and future collided in one urgent *now*, as animal instinct consumed them both. He found her heat, while she worked on his zip. Lifting her, he helped her to lock her legs around his waist. And then, glorious then, he drove his mouth down on hers and took her to the hilt. The relief was indescribable. They both exhaled loudly. Rosy came immediately with a series of screams that misted up the windows even more. Half-way up a mountain, with no one to hear them, she could be as abandoned as she liked. Rosy took full advantage of that. Her fingers gripped his buttocks as she worked him frantically and begged for more.

'I need this,' she commanded, driving him fast and hard. They were both dragging in air as if they were drowning until, throwing her head back, she came noisily again.

'Better now?' he suggested.

'Not nearly,' she complained, starting to move again.

'Oh, I suppose, if I must,' he teased.

He laughed deep and low, when she warned, 'You'd better.'

Some time later, when the summit of the mountain was in sight, Rosy loosened her death grip on his buttocks and gradually subsided against his chest.

'What just happened?' she murmured.

'A volcano erupted?' Making him more confident than ever that this...whatever *this* was, would quickly burn itself out.

'Was that all it was?' Rosy asked, and with the question something died in her eyes. It was as if a light had gone out.

He supposed he had been blunt, but the top station was almost upon them.

'Better straighten your clothes,' he advised. 'We're nearly there.'

'We've peaked?' Rosy observed dryly.

'Theos!' he exclaimed, raking his hair and, not for the first time, he wondered why he'd allowed himself to become involved with a woman like Rosy Boom.

Endlessly fascinating, and predictably infuriating, she was like a siren luring him onto the rocks. But even he couldn't be completely heartless, and with a brief, reassuring kiss on her mouth he helped her to straighten her clothes.

'Look at the view,' he said when this was done. Rubbing the steam off their window, he glanced outside. 'We're approaching the top of the glacier. Luckily, it's a clear day. You can see for miles from here.'

'Oh, that's wonderful,' she agreed, but the mood had changed and there was no pressing up against him, no contact at all, in fact. Rosy was far more self-possessed than any woman he'd known. No blushes from Rosy, no appeals for reassurance, no enquiry as to whether this would ever happen again. Just a gasp of honest wonder as she stared at the jagged peaks of the mountains surrounding them. 'It's like another world,' she said. 'No wonder you love your Swiss home so much.'

They waited in silence for the doors to open at the topmost station, Rosy no doubt wondering why he found it easier to love inanimate rock than another human being. Making sure Rosy found safe footing on the platform and ground, he guided her to the exit and the snowbound trails beyond.

CHAPTER THIRTEEN

So HE *WAS* going to dump her in a café. Rosy pulled a face behind Xander's back as he stopped in front of a rustic restaurant. What did she expect? Just because they'd had fabulous sex in a gondola didn't mean Xander had changed into some romantic version of himself.

Couldn't women enjoy sex for its own sake, just like men? She could. She would. She had. No, she hadn't, but at least she'd tried. Still, she reflected as he turned to make sure she was following him to the door, it would have been nice to spend some time together before Xander set off down the piste. Maybe it wasn't such a bad thing—maybe she needed recovery time on her own. Sex with Xander was off-the-scale amazing, but it left her feeling emotionally drained, as if all the light and warmth had been scooped out of her, to be replaced by passing pleasure. That wasn't supposed to happen, was it? Weren't you supposed to feel complete?

'Rosy?' Xander prompted, reminding her that he was still standing there, holding the door. 'Hungry?'

She thought about this for all of two seconds. 'Starving,' she admitted, suddenly realising it had been a long time since breakfast.

'The food here is really good,' he enthused, 'and I don't know about you, but I've built up quite an appetite.'

And no wonder, she thought, hiding a smile behind the straightest of faces.

'Hey—'

She started with surprise, realising that Xander was shooting warning glances at a group of youths who were making comments about Rosy as she walked past them. Then she remembered the glamorous designer sunglasses she was wearing that hid half her face, not to mention the fabulously expensive, high fashion skiwear. She hadn't wanted to make the most of herself ever since Achilles had pressed her down on that desk, but now, here with Xander, she was glad his PA had chosen such flattering outfits for her.

Xander led the way into the warmth of the mountain inn. Beautifully decorated in typical Swiss style, there were red and white gingham tablecloths, wood-lined walls and a roaring log fire. The crowd parted for Xander as if he were accompanied by an army of invisible bodyguards and then the manager rushed forward to guide them to what had to be the best table in the house. Overlooking mountains and the snow-carpeted pistes, it was a memory to cherish for ever. Xander had left his skis outside on a rack, so it surprised her to hear that he had a helmet ready for her to wear after they left the restaurant.

'What will I need that for, when I'm not going to ski?'

'You'll need it,' he said, turning his attention to the menu.

'I won't be skiing,' she said again, to make sure he'd heard.

Xander continued to study the menu. 'Okay,' he agreed mildly. 'By the way…' He glanced up with a searing stare into her eyes as he added, 'Do you know you're grinding your teeth?'

'Perhaps if you answered me…'

'What do you want me to say?'

Some mention of their time in the gondola—a look, a smile, a hint that it had meant more to him than a mechanical, if hugely enjoyable, encounter.

'What happens in the gondola stays in the gondola,' he intoned without expression. 'Is that what you need to hear?'

Not even close.

'No! *No!*' Rosy took a decisive step back as Xander held out the helmet. 'You've got to be joking!' she exclaimed with a longing glance towards the mountain inn they'd just left. 'Absolutely not! I'm not wearing that. I don't need to. I'll wait in the restaurant while you have your fun.'

'How will you get to my house?'

'I don't have to get to your house. I can go back down the mountain on the gondola.'

'And then?'

'I'll take a taxi to the hotel.'

'Do you have a ticket for the gondola?'

'No. But I can buy one. Failing that, I'll walk.'

'The gondola does go right over my house,' Xander reflected with a lift of his brow as he put on his own helmet. 'I guess you could parachute down.' With a shrug, he hunkered down to tighten the buckles on his ski boots. 'Now, stand on my skis,' he said, straightening up.

'What?' She looked at him askance.

'Stand on my skis,' he repeated. 'Come on, you'll be fine. My property is just a short way down the slope.'

'Like how far?' Sheer, unadulterated terror warred with intrigue and excitement. Xander planned to take her to his Swiss home. Yes, but in the most terrifying way imaginable. And, judging by his expression, not for a romantic tryst. So, what then? To discuss business? Her father? The school? All were equally important to Rosy, and he knew that.

'Stop looking so worried. I'll get you there safely.'

'Hmm.' She threw him a dubious look. Everyone had heard about Xander's mountaintop retreat, said to be the most desirable dwelling in Gstaad, and there was quite a bit of competition for that title. She wanted to go. Was curious to see inside. But... 'You do remember I can't ski?'

'But I can,' he countered with a relaxed shrug. 'Come on,' he encouraged. 'Prepare to be surprised.'

That was what she was frightened of!

'What do I do? Slide down, while you glide down the piste?'

'No. I take you with me. Put your helmet on, then come over here.'

After warily eyeing what looked like a cliff edge, she did as he asked. Maybe, if he skied really slowly, she'd be able to keep up?

'Well?' he prompted, frowning behind his stylish sunglasses. 'Are you going to join me, or are you going to stand there until you freeze?' He made a come-on gesture with his hand.

'I don't know what you want me to do,' she admitted.

'Here—I'll show you.' Skidding to within an inch of her toes, Xander brought her in front of him, on top of his skis. With her back pressed hard to his chest and Xander's arms wrapped firmly around her body, she barely had a chance to register what he was about to do when he set off down the slope.

'Relax. Enjoy yourself.' Xander's breath was hot on that part of her neck the helmet had failed to cover. 'Look around. Don't worry, I'll keep you safe—'

If anyone could, he could, but that didn't make it any easier to accept that they were flying down a mountain with an ever-steeper drop looming in front of them. Gritting her teeth, she braced herself for disaster as he weaved a path through less capable skiers.

Rejoice! She was still alive. And able to look around and enjoy the view. The rush of speed, together with the sensation of moving as one, was exhilarating. And yes, she felt safe in his arms. Xander was an expert at this, as he was in so many other things—though she would not think about those things now, not while she was flying, or at least it felt as if she was. The only remaining question was if Xander was giving her this amazing experience because it was the quickest way to get to his chalet, or if he was actually doing it because he enjoyed it too.

With their bodies completely in sync, and only their clothes dividing them, it was hard to stop her mind straying onto the dark side. It was almost a relief when

Xander slowed suddenly, throwing up a great plume of snow as he turned sideways onto the slope.

'Welcome,' he said, lifting his helmet's visor.

They had halted outside a huge and impressive Swiss chalet.

'This is yours?' Photographs in magazines weren't even close to doing it justice.

'It is,' he confirmed, adding, 'You can get off my skis now—'

And now she didn't want to. She could have stayed where she was for the rest of her life, with Xander's arms wrapped securely around her.

'I'd love to do that again some time,' she admitted. 'I'd like to learn to ski. You must have given me the bug. Right, okay—I'll get off,' she said, seeing his expression.

The chalet was like a Swiss-style palace in size, and yet the interior was cosy and inviting. A steeply pitched roof with towering front gables and wide eaves supported by decorative brackets, most of which had hearts carved deep into the wood, prompted her to ask, 'Did you design this?'

'I had a hand in it,' Xander admitted as he led her into what, he explained, was the boot room.

'Hmm. So you *are* a secret romantic?'

He stared down at her with a frown of bemusement. 'No. I love all things Swiss.'

Okay.

When they went into the main house Rosy could only gasp when she caught sight of the extraordinary view. Framed by floor-to-ceiling windows, the town far below looked like a model village, with towering mountain peaks, crowned by fluffy pink clouds, standing timeless and majestic behind.

'You're a lucky man,' she murmured, too entranced to turn around.

'Yes, I am,' Xander agreed, his gaze on the magical snow scene outside, she finally noticed—just in case she had thought he might be looking at her.

Having Rosy beside him in one of his favourite homes felt good—made him think about happier times with Eleni and Romanos. Whenever they'd come to stay he'd light a fire, open the wine for Eleni and share a beer with Romanos, while they gave Eleni a rest and spread a feast of tempting local fare on the dining table. He hadn't become a hermit since they'd died; there had been visitors, but no one had lightened his mood like Rosy. But a lot of water had passed under that bridge, and although she was enjoying herself—the gondola, the skiing, the lunch, the house—he could sense she was still wary of him. Who could blame her? He was hardly noted for his constancy where women were concerned.

'Hungry?'

'Yes,' she admitted, frowning with surprise. 'It seems an age since we ate that fondue.'

'It's the fresh mountain air. What can I get you? Beer? Wine? Champagne?'

'Water, please.'

Yes. Wary. He congratulated himself on reading Rosy correctly.

'Would you care to follow me?' He said this lightly, and she did follow, but at a distance, leaving him to conclude that ski-type adventures were all very well, while finding herself alone in his house was something quite different for Rosy.

'I didn't have you pegged as a home-maker,' she admitted, still keeping her distance as she stared around the kitchen, most notably the crammed inside of his fridge.

'Not me—Astrid. My housekeeper,' he explained, straightening up after selecting a bunch of fresh produce. 'She sees to everything.'

'Does everyone spoil you?'

'Not you,' he said dryly.

'That must make a nice change for you.'

'I'm not complaining.'

And then she made her first mistake.

'This—' she gestured around '—must be quite a contrast to your childhood?'

'Some.' The mood had immediately changed. She had changed it, and he doubted it could be saved. 'I don't know why you'd say that.'

Realising her blunder, she backtracked calmly. 'Sorry—I was thinking about your early life with Eleni and Romanos...'

'Of course,' he allowed tensely. 'What else could you mean?' Not those years of scrabbling for something to eat, or fighting to keep warm in the winter. 'Let's not go there, Rosy. My early life is not something I choose to discuss.'

'Perhaps you should.' Her words hung in the air like the ringing of a bell. And then she said softly, 'Please...'

'You don't need to hear the details; the tabloids have raked over it incessantly.'

'But maybe you need to speak it out loud for yourself—exorcise the demons?'

'All right.' She'd asked for it. Perhaps this would show Rosy once and for all that there might be an electric attraction between them, but there could never be anything long-term. 'I appreciated what Eleni and Romanos did for me, more than I could ever say—'

'Root cause of guilt number one,' Rosy murmured thoughtfully.

'Are you going to listen, or are you going to comment all the way through?'

'Sorry. I didn't mean to interrupt. Please—go on...'

'I never knew my birth parents. I was told that my father was a true Romani, and that my mother sneaked away from the brothel where she worked, late at night, to meet up with him, which was why, when she went into labour with me, the owner of the brothel had no sympathy with her. She'd cost him valuable clients, her friends told me, and so the owner left her to it. By denying her the most basic medical care, he let her die.'

'That's horrendous.'

'Yes.'

He tried to make light of the past with a rueful shrug, but neither of them was fooled. Xander's story was a tragedy beyond imagining, both for him and for his mother.

'I would have been thrown out with the rubbish if my mother's friends hadn't hidden me and cared for me in their own way. But none of them stayed around for long as they had their own troubles. There was a constantly changing cast of sad, vulnerable women in that brothel.'

'Which inevitably meant your care was patchy,' Rosy guessed.

'Whoever was in residence at the time had so little, but they shared what they could with me.'

He indicated a seat at the breakfast bar, but they both preferred to remain standing as Rosy mused, 'Hence your philanthropic nature. That's you, showing your appreciation for what those women did for you, and wanting to pay it forward later on.'

He stopped her there. 'Would you like to tell the rest of the story?'

She lifted her chin. 'Sorry.' Her emerald gaze remained steady on his face. But she couldn't contain herself. 'Those women passed through your life like so many butterflies, never able to stay for long, and that's all you knew, so now you believe you can never let anyone in, because the sad fate of those women is ingrained in you. You probably feel you don't deserve love...'

'When I need a therapy session, I'll ask for one.'

'Sorry,' she said again, but there was a new knowledge in her eyes, a new certainty.

He had to dislodge that before it took root.

'You deserve a straightforward man with a straightforward background, Rosy.'

'You don't know what I deserve, and you certainly don't make my decisions for me,' she said bluntly. 'Shall I make the coffee?' she added, no doubt to soften her remark.

It wasn't Rosy's fault he had an Achilles heel when it came to his past. His early life always provoked rage inside him, which was why he had opened orphanages across Greece with the aim of rescuing street children and placing them in happy homes across the world. Romanos had shown him the way in so many things, and if Xander had failed to demonstrate his gratitude with the emotion he kept bottled inside him, at least he had made sufficient money to be able to save countless children like himself.

Rosy had also suffered her fair share of knockbacks, knowing both grief and abandonment within a short space of time. But she hadn't had the luxury of growing up streetwise as he had, and had instead learned to survive as she went along.

'I'm really sorry if I've upset you,' she said as she passed him a mug of strong black coffee. 'I, of all people, should know how it hurts to look back. While I had a wonderful childhood, you didn't know where your next meal was coming from—'

'But that privilege left you ill-equipped to deal with your mother dying, and then your father putting your stepmother before you, which must have been a crushing blow.'

'It was,' she admitted bluntly, 'but I couldn't sit around feeling sorry for myself. I had to get on with things, and make a new life for myself.'

'Which you've done.'

'Which we've both done,' she corrected him levelly.

He ground his jaw at the thought that Rosy knew him better than anyone, and that didn't please him because he knew he'd only let her down and hurt her in the end.

'Why don't we take coffee and snacks into the other room?' he suggested.

Once they were settled, he said something he'd been longing to say. 'It must have taken a great deal of courage to strike out on your own while you were still griev-ing for your mother. I admire you,' he admitted.

'Does that mean I get to keep my job?'

She said this lightly, but there was real concern be-hind her eyes.

'For as long as you want it,' he pledged.

'Thank you—I mean that. The job means a lot to me.'

She didn't need to tell him that. 'No need to thank me.'

'I think there is,' she argued gently. And then, after a pause, she stared at him directly and admitted. 'Only if you want to tell me...but I'd love to hear more about Eleni and Romanos, from your point of view.'

He flinched as guilt hit him all over again. 'I'll never forgive myself,' he murmured, hardly aware that he was talking out loud.

'For what?' Rosy pressed. 'What's weighing you down? I've shared my secrets—'

'And I've shared mine,' he said, hoping that was an end to the subject.

'But you haven't shared the reason for your guilt,' Rosy pointed out with her usual forthrightness.

'All right,' he said with a casual shrug, as if none of his memories mattered at all. 'I put work above staying longer on the island, which would have allowed Roma-nos to get over his grief at Eleni's death.'

'He would never get over that,' Rosy said with con-fidence.

'But it was me who gave Achilles a foothold into terrorising the islanders and, eventually, driving both himself and Romanos off a cliff.'

'That wasn't your fault, it was his,' she insisted. 'I don't know what you could have done to stop him.'

Maybe nothing, he reflected, thinking back to what a determined, treacherous snake Achilles had been. Was she right? Even if Rosy was only partly right, it was a form of absolution—something to cling to when the guilt struck him particularly hard. She'd taken a weight off his soul, he realised, allowing that to sink in for a moment.

'Tell me more about yourself,' he said at last. 'Has the pain over your mother's death lessened? Can you face your emotions now?'

'Who says I couldn't before?'

The lift of one brow was his answer.

'Says the man who never shows his feelings,' Rosy countered with a level stare.

'Is that really how you see me?'

'It really is,' she confirmed, gazing at him over the rim of her coffee mug. 'Your default setting is "need to know".'

'While yours is "back off"?' he suggested. 'Do you think it's time to declare a truce?'

'Tell me first how Romanos found you.'

He shrugged. 'With the ever-revolving door at the brothel, there was no one to protect a child from predatory men—'

'Pimps and drug dealers,' she interrupted with alarm.

'And perverts galore,' he supplied. 'It was easier—almost safer—on the streets.'

'And that's where Romanos found you?'

'My guardian angel.'

'Mine too,' Rosy murmured.

'Seems we have more in common than we thought.'

'You know, there's nothing, absolutely nothing, you could have done to stop Achilles behaving as he did.'

'You're my counsellor now?'

'I'd say we're helping each other, aren't we?'

This was the first time he'd talked about the past without those memories stabbing him. Enjoying conversation outside of sex with a woman was novel too. They'd both made themselves vulnerable with the revelations they'd shared. Better still, Rosy seemed far less wary of him. Gentle and relaxed, she appeared genuinely interested. How shallow and pointless his other lovers seemed now.

Their faces had grown close as they talked, so close they shared the same breath, the same air. It was only natural to close the final distance between them, and when they kissed it felt like the most natural thing in the world. There was no rush, no reaching and grabbing, just an inevitable coming together to share the most tender and cherishing of moments.

Nuzzling his lips against Rosy's, he smiled and teased and pulled away before returning to apply a little more pressure. He waited until she was ready and parted her lips under his, before kissing her deeply, and even then it was very different to anything they'd shared before, as if everything they'd talked about had broken down a barrier.

CHAPTER FOURTEEN

ROSY HADN'T REALISED until that exact moment that desire could hold such an emotional charge. She'd never felt anything like it before, not even when earthy, primitive desire for Xander had consumed her completely. This was different, better, better by far—better still for sensing that he felt it too. She could feel Xander's restraint, his respect and care for her and, beneath that, his desire. They brushed lips and kissed for the longest time, teasing each other by pulling away, only to return for more kisses, until holding back was no longer possible.

'So many clothes,' Xander complained, smiling against her mouth as she set about releasing his zip. When they were naked, or naked enough, he put on protection, then took her gently and deeply, without foreplay or hesitation. Only mutual acceptance that this was right allowed them to join as one, move as one, and as the world, with all its complications, slipped away, Xander held her wrists in a loose grip on the cushions above her head, pleasuring her with complete focus and concentration, leaving no question in Rosy's mind that their physical pleasure had moved onto a different plane, where emotion and trust between them was as important as sensation.

When Rosy cried out her release in his arms, Xander experienced a surge of pleasure unlike any he'd known before. When she demanded more, he knew he could never get enough of her. When the storm subsided, he kissed her again.

'Have I ever told you how amazing you are?' she murmured in a contented tone.

'Once or twice,' he admitted tongue-in-cheek.

'Usually in bed?' she suggested.

'I have noticed a pattern emerging.' He dropped a kiss on her brow as he smiled into her eyes. 'But I wouldn't change a thing.'

'Really?' she whispered with so much trust in her eyes that he instinctively flinched and pulled back.

What was he doing to this woman? Could he live with himself when it was over? Everything good came to an end eventually.

'Really,' he assured her through a thickened throat. 'Since you judging me amazing always seems to happen after sex.'

He saw the flicker in her eyes and knew that what they'd done *again* had meant so much more to her than that.

'That's not the case,' she argued half seriously, half not. 'Because now I've had time to think.'

'And what is your conclusion?' he whispered, staring down.

'You're amazing,' she said, curbing the smile on her mouth. 'And that is all.'

He had to huff a laugh at that, and then she pulled away to straighten her clothes.

Padding to the window, she took a look at the snow scene outside. 'I've never been anywhere like this before,' she admitted. 'It's so beautiful.' And before he could answer that she added, 'I've never met anyone like you before.'

He found himself thinking, *Thank God for that.*

Swinging around, she explained, 'I want to imprint all this on my mind for ever.'

In case she never saw this house, or him, again? He could pretend he was happy about that, but he was what he was, and he was unlikely to change now.

Rearranging himself, he stood and went to join her. 'It's been a long day. Let's go to bed.'

She looked at him and hesitated for a moment, but then, as if deciding that this was what she wanted, really wanted, whatever the cost, she smiled and followed him to his bedroom.

'Wow, you must be a brilliant polo player,' she commented at one point, spotting a picture of him playing on the Acosta team. 'Aren't they the best players in the world?' Turning to him, she added, 'Is there anything you can't do?'

So much when it came to this woman.

Pressing his lips down in pretend contemplation, he offered, 'I can't slice a loaf of bread with a banana.'

She laughed, and that was Rosy's cue to take hold of his hand and link their fingers. It was such a little thing, but it made him feel warm too. Turning her face up to his, she looked at him for several long moments, and then laughed again.

'Who knew the great Xander Tsakis had a sense of humour beneath his steely armour? I think we're almost in danger of getting to know each other.'

'Perhaps,' he conceded with a good-natured shrug. But this was as far as it must go, because he had nothing to offer Rosy apart from a good time and sex. And money, though he doubted that that would ever impress her.

'Don't do that,' she called after him as he started to walk away.

'Don't do what?' he asked, pausing.

'Shut down, close off, just when I think we're becoming close.'

That was what he was most afraid of.

'I can see I've gone too far,' she said as she drew alongside. 'Let's just settle for this—it will be easier to work for you, now I know a little more about you.'

Was she content to settle for that? Relief and disappointment swept over him in successive waves. Rosy would soon return to the island, he would continue to roam around the globe, and it would be as if this had never happened.

All the more reason to enjoy the time they had left.

'One more question,' she said with a hand on his arm as he was about to lead the way into his bedroom. 'Did you ever get on with Achilles?'

'In between him torturing animals and calling me a dirty gypsy, do you mean?'

'I'm sorry, Xander. I didn't mean to upset you.'

'You just had to know.'

'Yes,' Rosy admitted frankly. 'I just had to know.'

'In case there were any similarities between us? Let

me reassure you, there are none. Achilles was always spoiled and out of control.'

'So Romanos brought you into the family to…?'

'For no other reason than Romanos was a good man.'

'But Achilles could never accept Romanos's decision to include you in the family?'

'You could say that—'

'Xander,' she said, catching hold of his sleeve as he opened the door to his room. 'What did Achilles do to you?'

'You don't want to know—'

'But I do,' she insisted, maintaining her grip on his sleeve. 'Don't let that monster ruin your life.'

Planting his fist on the door, he bowed his head as the memories came sweeping back. He was nine years old, in the Big House kitchen with Eleni and Romanos, tears pouring down his face. 'One of the worst things he did was drown the stable cat's kittens I'd been caring for,' he rapped out now to Rosy, afraid to show how he still felt about that in case he broke down. Grown men didn't do that kind of thing, especially not men like Xander Tsakis. 'I used to spend time with the mother cat as she nursed her kittens, confiding things I couldn't even tell to Eleni and Romanos, like the beatings in the brothel, and the fear the women lived with. I used to wonder about my mother and hope she hadn't suffered too much. Though, of course, her pimp couldn't resist telling me over and over again that I'd killed her when she gave birth to me. It was only later I found out that his spite had killed her, because he refused to pay for the care she had needed after my birth, with the excuse that she hadn't earned her keep while she'd been carrying me.'

'What a hideous fate for your poor mother.' Rosy's voice broke with pity. 'But you weren't to blame for that. And Achilles was a monster, while you're a good man.'

'Am I?' he said hollowly.

'Yes,' she stated firmly. 'You are.'

The memory of finding the mother cat and her kittens lined up in a soggy parody of the playtime they'd used to enjoy made him flinch even now, especially when Achilles' sneering, laughing face stole into his mind. He had never once wished Achilles dead, not even then, but if only fate had stepped in sooner then maybe Romanos would still be alive—

'No, Xander, no,' Rosy exclaimed, seeing the fury and pain in his eyes. 'You're so much better than Achilles. Don't let the past distract you now. Let it go.'

They shared an impassioned look, then he swept Rosy off her feet and carried her into his bedroom.

Everything Xander had ever loved had been taken away from him, Rosy reflected as they took a shower in his bathroom after they'd made love. They were familiar with each other's bodies so there was no embarrassment on her part as warm water spilled over them. It was a cleansing process in more ways than one. They didn't speak, they just allowed the steam and warmth to bathe them in a sense of wellbeing.

'I understand you better now,' she said at last.

'Oh?' Xander slanted her an enigmatic look. He'd never been more beautiful in Rosy's eyes than he was now. Naked and powerful, and yet he'd finally shown her a tender side, and it was that side she found most beguiling.

'You've helped me to understand why you're so mistrustful when it comes to risking your heart.'

'Is your heart in danger?' he asked as he handed her a towel, securing one around his waist.

'Is yours?' she countered, holding his stare steadily.

'When it is, I'll let you know.'

Did she expect him to change and tell her that he loved her? No, Rosy reasoned as Xander dried off and tugged on his jeans, but that didn't change the fact that she was in love with him—completely in love…hopelessly in love. But now she wondered if the tenderness he'd shown towards her was pity. Was she guilty of being gullible to think Xander had brought her here to his beautiful house to do anything other than have sex?

'Rosy?' He'd turned at the door.

'Yes?'

He frowned. 'You look so wounded.'

Xander seemed genuinely concerned, but how could she not feel wounded—at her own failings far more than his? Some people were charismatic, while Xander had the type of animal magnetism that could drive lemmings off a cliff, but that was no excuse for Rosy to become one of them. She had free will and could make her own decisions.

'It's time I went home,' she said with a glance at her watch.

'You are home,' Xander insisted.

'I mean, back home to the hotel,' she explained. 'It's been a hell of a day, and I'm tired.' Her soul was tired, her body was tired and her mind was utterly exhausted from trying to find an escape route from her love for this man.

'Why go back to the hotel when you can sleep here?' Xander asked with a puzzled frown.

Because she'd already slept in his bed, in his arms, which had only allowed the fantasy of happy ever after to grow. She might be many things, but a glutton for punishment wasn't one of them.

'None of the other bedrooms are made up, but you can stay in my bed. No,' Xander added, seeing her expression. 'I mean you can take my bed while I sleep on the couch.'

'I can't let you do that.' But was it fair to drag him out to take her back to the hotel? Belting her robe, she followed him into the Great Room.

'Staying here is the sensible thing to do,' Xander remarked as he glanced out of the window at the falling snow. 'Plus, bedroom or Great Room, we'll both have an excellent view of the most spectacular event on the mountain. A torchlit procession,' he explained when she gave him an enquiring look.

'I hope you're not missing out on something because of me?'

'I begged you to leave—'

They looked at each other for a moment, and then Xander's mouth curved, and she began to laugh. And, of course, tears threatened. She wanted to laugh, she wanted to cry; she'd never felt so vulnerable before. Half of her wanted him to stop teasing, while the other half never wanted him to stop smiling into her eyes like that.

Xander had not exaggerated when he'd talked about a spectacle. Now she could see the line of skiers carrying torches from the top of the mountain, weaving a snaking path down the slope. It was like a dream when they drifted past the window—a dream from which she never wanted to wake up. They stayed to watch until the last light had been swallowed up in the town far below. She almost laughed then, at the parallel of that stream of light, so bold and fierce, dwindling until it had completely disappeared, pretty much like passion.

'I don't want to put you out. I really should be getting back—'

'No, it'll be crazy in town. Everyone will be partying when the skiers get back. You'll get a much better night's sleep if you stay here. You won't be disturbed. I'll take the couch. You know where my bedroom is. Make yourself at home.'

After making love it felt odd to sleep alone, but it was far safer for a heart that couldn't take much more battering. After that romantic ski down the mountain, followed by the torchlit parade of skiers, she might have expected them to continue to talk long into the night, after the opening up that had already happened, but no, she was alone in Xander's stylish bedroom. This was his private space, his spartan quarters, where everything was of the finest quality, with no frivolous extras, not even a photograph to clutter the expensive surfaces. It was as if a wealthy monk had put his print on the bedroom. That was Xander, the sexy monk with more hidden depths than Rosy, or anyone else, could ever hope to plumb.

On that thought, she climbed into bed—Xander's bed, where she would sleep alone. Dragging the covers over her, she squeezed her eyes shut and concentrated on the memory of a long trail of light disappearing down a mountainside until each glowing torch was finally extinguished, in a Swiss version of counting sheep.

How could a couch that was so comfortable by day make such a lousy bed?

He'd have to put up with it.

He couldn't put up with it.

Maybe Rosy would allow him to share his own bed, he reflected with a wry, and not entirely innocent smile on his face.

Rosy woke slowly the next day, not really sure where she was. Switzerland. Her heart leapt at the thought. It was such a beautiful country. Dawn was peeping through the curtains, promising a snow-kissed, sunny day. Inhaling deeply, she felt a deep sense of contentment... For precisely two seconds.

'*What the—? What are you doing here?*' A yowl of shock sprang from her throat as she leapt out of bed. Holding a pillow defensively in front of her, she watched as Xander stretched lazily.

'*Theós*, Rosy! I thought there was a fire for a moment there.'

A naked Xander! A naked Xander had been lying next to her in the bed all night?

Oh, if he hadn't been so magnificent...

She'd have what? Had sex with him yet again?

'Are you okay?' he drawled huskily, one powerful forearm resting over his face.

Now she'd found a robe to drag on, yes.

'I thought you were sleeping on the sofa?'

'I made a rubbish choice. It was clearly designed by a sadist.'

'I'm sorry I took your bed.'

'Hmm, so you should be.'

He didn't sound annoyed, he sounded sexy.

'We only slept together,' he pointed out, sitting up to stare her way. 'You looked so cute and innocent lying there, I didn't want to disturb you.'

Cute? Innocent? Neither descriptor suited her mood. He hadn't even been tempted to wake her.

Great. Good. Maybe now they could get that employer/ employee relationship back on track.

'I slept well,' Xander observed with an acknowledging nod. 'Trust you did too?'

She should count herself lucky to have spent the night with such a principled man, not be longing for bad Xander, the man who made her body ache with lust. But how was she supposed to do that when, sleep-tousled and as thickly stubbled as a mountain man, he looked so sexy?

'Are you coming back to bed?'

'Only if you're getting out of it,' she countered, feeling a buzz of want, having noticed the wicked smile playing around his firm mouth. 'I'll take a shower.'

Great idea. She'd proved, to herself at least, that she could be strong.

Her triumph was short-lived. Barely had she turned her face up to the spray when a naked Xander joined her.

'What are you doing?' Acting outraged was hard when he was hard, and when she wanted him so badly.

He shrugged lazily. 'I'm taking a shower.' Boxing

her in with his fists planted either side of her face on the black marble tiles, he dipped his head to tease her mouth with kisses.

'What you're doing is taking an unfair advantage.'

He hummed at this, and seemed to agree. 'Would you like me to leave?'

'What a flagrant waste of water,' she protested.

He smiled wickedly and, keeping her gaze confined to his face, she invited, 'Soap?'

'You'd like me to wash you?'

'Did I say that?'

'You didn't need to.'

So now she was lost.

Using a sponge, he soaped her down with impressive attention to detail. His skilful touch, in a space that was intimate and steamy, completed her seduction. Until he stopped. And proceeded to wash himself down with the efficiency of a sergeant major on parade. When that was done he announced, 'I'm going for a swim now. You can join me if you want to.'

Stung by his casual offer, she was quick to refuse. 'No, that's okay—'

Too late. He'd gone.

Rinsing the soap out of her hair, she turned off the shower. Why had he gone? Had Xander finally had enough of her? Did her naked body turn him off now? It certainly hadn't seemed like that while he was soaping her down, quite the contrary in fact. So what was going on in his head?

What was he trying to prove? That he was ready for the monastery? No. The intimacy of the shower, that warm cocoon enclosing them both after a night spent lying by her side, had almost broken his resolve not to let things progress too far with Rosy, in case he hurt her. Why couldn't he just enjoy the sex and leave it at that? Why must it always turn into something deeper with her? The chill of the water in his swimming pool had no answers, and did nothing to ease his frustration. He was still as hard as he'd been in the shower. If she did decide to join him she'd get a shock.

'*Wow!*'

He spun around in the water at the sound of her voice.

'You're here,' he said with surprise.

'Your pool's Olympic-size. I couldn't resist,' she said as she slipped into the water beside him.

'Did you not bring a swimming costume?'

'Oh, yes, I packed one for skiing,' she teased, but then her expression changed. 'You sound tense. Is everything okay?'

Yes, if he stayed in the pool until Rosy got out. There was no way to hide how she made him feel. It was safer for her if he kept the relationship simmering until the heat gradually died away than allow it to keep roaring into an inferno. Too many times doing that and there would be serious emotional consequences, for Rosy at least.

'Are you sure you're okay?' she asked with concern as they reached the side of the pool.

'Fine.' Not fine. Something had to give. And that something manifested itself in five succinct words. 'Why are you wearing underwear?'

She half laughed, and looked at him in bemusement.

'Take it off.'

'I beg your pardon?'

'You heard me.'

Rosy studied him, as if assessing her options, and then her eyes darkened and her lips plumped as she obeyed.

'There,' he approved. 'Doesn't that feel better?'

He didn't expect an answer, but she gave him one anyway. Linking her arms around his neck, she pressed her body against his as she whispered, 'Much better.'

Nuzzling her neck with the lightest brush of his stubble made her whimper with desire, and she soon made it clear she wanted more. Nudging his way between her thighs, he gave her the tip of his erection.

'I need a lot more than that,' she told him with a long stare into his eyes.

Lifting her so her legs were floating in the water, he arranged her to his liking. 'Better?'

'A lot better, but still not enough—' The breath caught in her throat as he took her deep. 'That's good,' she approved. 'I hope you're in for the long haul. Control is your middle name, isn't it?' she teased in between gasping for breath.

'It is,' he confirmed. 'As you are about to discover.'

CHAPTER FIFTEEN

SHE WAS STILL floating in an erotic haze when they got dressed and left the pool house for the main room with its ceiling of stars.

Rosy knew there were parts of Xander she would never be allowed to share, but if she could have this closeness with him, for however short a time, before their boss and employee status was put back firmly in place, she'd take it. While they'd been here in the mountains she'd seen a different side of Xander, and it had given her a glimpse of happiness, knowing he could be freer and more uninhibited.

Taking her for that ski run down the slope had been thrilling and exhilarating, leaving her in no doubt that here in his mountain eyrie Xander's barriers were definitely down. She loved to see him like this. She loved the intent look in his eyes, the power of his mind, and his incredible physicality. The pleasure he could bring her with one kiss was incalculable.

As if to prove her right, he pulled her close and kissed her deep, kissing her as if he meant it…as if he really, *really* meant it. Was it foolish to take a sliver of hope from that? Was it possible that one day Xander might truly relax and learn to love and to trust again? He was so different right now, she dared to hope that this time it might last.

And then his phone rang.

'I'm sorry, I've got to take this,' he said, frowning at the screen as he walked away.

'Of course.' What else could she say? But something deep inside her said that the moment they'd shared had gone, lost for ever, with no way of bringing it back.

This was bad. She listened as Xander rattled off a few instructions, and then turned around to face her. He'd explain. She'd understand. With business commitments as numerous as his, as well as his charitable work, it was inevitable that Xander would never stay in one place too long. He was a decisive man, no dithering, which his next words confirmed.

'I'm sorry, something important has come up and I have to leave immediately. You can, of course, stay on here for as long as you want.'

Rosy felt as if her head was exploding. Nothing had changed at all. Xander was the same man who would always put business above everything else. He had an established history of doing this, so she was the fool for hoping, even for an instant, that he might change his ways for her.

Composing her face, she said, 'That's very kind of you, but as the clinic said it would be better for my father if he could have the chance to complete his therapy before seeing visitors, I don't see any reason to stay on in Switzerland. As soon as he's given the all-clear, I'll come back to take him home.'

'To Praxos?'

'Well, he doesn't have a house to go home to in England at the moment,' she reminded them both with a shrug. 'I think the sea air and warmth on Praxos would do him good, so yes, I'll take him back to the island with me.'

Xander's expression revealed absolutely nothing of the way he felt about this. That was if he even felt anything at all. She could never be more than a transient form of entertainment for him, and even that would change when they were back on Praxos, where Xander was her boss, and she was just the local teacher.

'Is it such a terrible prospect, to stay on here at the chalet until I get back? You'll be far more comfortable than at the hotel, and Astrid will love the company. I'm not quitting the planet, Rosy. This is just another short business trip.'

Xander expected her to hang around until he could find time in his schedule to see her again? Did he think her so needy? Surely she had more self-respect than that? She needed more than he was prepared to offer her—no, she *deserved* more. And if Xander couldn't give her that, then she should end this…whatever it was between them now, before she got even more hurt.

'I'm always contactable,' he added.

'Always contactable? Like you disappear for months at a time? Forgive me if my expectations aren't set too high.'

'And while your father's in the clinic,' Xander continued, as if she hadn't spoken, 'I've asked my PA, Peter, to keep an eye on you. Peter's available twenty-four-seven, so you'll have ready access to any help you might need.'

'I don't need *any* help,' she said pointedly, about to

add, *I'd appreciate your help.* The idea of some man she didn't know 'keeping an eye on her' was insulting, but she had to balance this against staying close to her father. What if he called? What if he didn't like the clinic? She couldn't abandon him now. She was almost ready to agree to Xander's plan when he brought out a thick wad of bank notes.

'This should be enough,' he said, 'but if you need more money Peter will wire whatever is required directly into your bank account.'

Mentally, she reeled. Shocked and inexpressibly hurt, she would readily admit that she didn't have much, but what little money she did have, she had earned honestly. What was this money for? Services rendered?

'I don't need your money, thank you,' she said icily.

'I can't allow you to be out of pocket. It was my idea to bring your father to Switzerland. Please do stay here instead of going back to the hotel. Astrid will take very good care of you, and you're due a break. What better time to take that break than now, when you can be close to your father in the most beautiful surroundings imaginable?'

Everything he said made perfect sense, but the bottom line…? Xander was leaving. Again.

Vicious curses bombarded his mind as he sat in his jet, heading for New York. He should have taken Rosy with him—would have done if things had been different, if she had been different—if she hadn't carved a place for herself in his cold, stony heart. He had to put an end to whatever this was between them, before he ruined her life. That was really why he was taking this trip alone.

He was turning his back on emotion. How did the prospect of life without Rosy make him feel? Empty didn't begin to describe how it felt. Even putting thousands of miles between them had failed to eject her from his mind. She was still here with him—her smile, her challenges, her humour and her heart, all of it underlining the fact that either he had to change or get out of her life.

Which is it to be, Xander?

He couldn't lose her. Praxos couldn't afford to lose her. Romanos would never have forgiven him if he drove her away. He wouldn't forgive himself if he kept her on the island to live out a life without her own children. How selfish would that be?

This trip to New York wasn't all about business. He would be visiting a school he hoped Rosy would join him in furthering Romanos's goal to promote education across the world. He needed Rosy's magic touch to make a success of it, but hadn't told her yet because he wanted to make sure in his own mind that this was right for Rosy. Yes, he needed her, but was fostering global education what she wanted to do with her life? He had to be sure of that first.

This felt like a crossroads. The direction he took would impact on both their lives. Could he change? Could he change enough? It had taken him a long time to trust Romanos and Eleni...

And they had left him too...

Stop thinking about yourself! Think about Rosy. If he ended this—whatever *this* was—his life would continue on, in the same affluent rut. And she'd be okay. He'd make sure she'd never want for anything.

Do you really think that's what Rosy wants?

He reassured himself that Rosy was quite capable of looking after herself. But could he go on without her? A glimpse of his life going forward alone looked like...

Cursing viciously beneath his breath, he conceded that it looked grim.

Yet he'd done the right thing, leaving before he broke her heart.

Hadn't he?

Yes. Rosy wouldn't leave her father. She would be waiting for him when he got back to Switzerland. They'd sort something out then. This was a vital cooling-down period, but he was certain she'd see the sense in his plan to concentrate on the good they could do together in Greece, in New York and elsewhere, furthering education for vulnerable children going forward.

There was no point staying in Switzerland now her father had been given a clean bill of health. He should come back for yearly check-ups, the therapists had suggested, or they could suggest a clinic more conveniently at hand.

'Praxos,' she'd said immediately. Why couldn't Xander build a facility like this on the island, or even somewhere close by on the mainland?

Her father's recovery had been nothing short of miraculous. He'd put this down to long snow-shoe walks in the crisp, clean Swiss air, as well as gardening, which had become his new hobby, he explained as they prepared to leave the clinic for the last time.

'There are several greenhouses on site where they propagate tender plants, ready to sow in the spring,' he explained. 'Watching those tiny shoots grow, and nurturing them, has taken over my life. Xander even gave me a special journal to keep a note of what I've learned,' he revealed as the cab Rosy had ordered pulled up outside the clinic.

'Xander did that?' Rosy exclaimed with surprise.

When her father confirmed this, she realised there were still so many sides to Xander she had yet to discover. If only he could share things with her—trust her, tell her, confide in her. Did he still think she would hurt him, abandon him, like all the rest, when nothing could be further from the truth?

Enlightenment rendered her silent as the cab weaved its way through the busy town on its way to the international airport. Xander Tsakis, totem to all things powerful and commanding, still had the ghost of a small, abandoned child inside him. If someone didn't exorcise that ghost for good, he would never be happy.

Once again she'd had no contact with him, and it seemed like for ever since she'd seen him last, but it was actually three weeks, two days, seven hours, six minutes and counting. Leaving was the right thing to do. She couldn't stay on in Switzerland indefinitely and now her father was finally feeling well enough to travel. The climate on Praxos would do him good and, she smiled at the thought, there would be countless gardens for him to work on. She had to go back too. She was needed at the school. And Rosy needed Praxos and her friends.

She'd had an amazing time in Switzerland, she reflected as their aircraft soared into the sky. It was just sad that she hadn't been able to reach Xander in the way that she'd hoped she could. She felt sorry for him, and wished she could have helped him to see that owning residences in so many different countries, without being able to call even one of them home, not even the one on Praxos, which Achilles had tainted with his cruelty, was sad. Would he ever know a real family home? she wondered as she stared out of the small aircraft window at the carpet of white clouds below. With all the good he did across the world, Xander deserved a family and someone to love. But he had chosen the world of business instead, and she doubted that would bring him very much comfort.

Was that really all he wanted? There was so much more to discover about Xander, but Rosy doubted she'd ever get the chance. Just as well, since her heart was hurting so badly it felt bruised. Better to concentrate on her father, the school children she loved and all the other islanders who had been so kind to her, rather than waste another second of her life dreaming about a man who had no intention of changing.

Her father distracted her, excitedly reminding her to fasten her seat belt. 'We're about to land on Praxos,' he enthused.

'Yes, Dad.' Clutching his arm, she pressed her cheek fondly against his. 'And you're on the brink of starting a wonderful new life.'

She'd really gone?

Yes. And who could blame her? Did he really think Rosy would have waited for him once her father's treatment was completed? Hadn't he done this before, walking out with scarcely a word of explanation and no contact? He'd never felt the need to explain before, and no woman had ever demanded that of him, but Rosy was different. She didn't demand, or make a fuss, but that didn't make the way he treated her right. Rosy's silence and her absence was his punishment. Her strength in the face of his neglect was his shame.

He couldn't rest. The opulent rooms of his Swiss chalet, so recently full of Rosy's vitality, seemed gloomy now. He missed her laughter, her common sense, her good ideas. Most of all, he missed Rosy. Thoughtful and caring for everyone around her, she had remained positive in the face of every setback she'd faced, and there had been more than a few. Rosy's overriding determination throughout had remained with one goal in mind: find a way to push on and make things better for all. While he had somehow become a destroyer of all things good. She'd tried to show him that she cared about him, while he had acted as he always had, running away as soon as business came calling. Astrid's best attempts to soothe him had fallen flat. Nothing pleased him. He paced the floor of the chalet until Astrid suggested he'd wear it out.

Nothing would be right until he saw Rosy again and reassured her that he had listened, he did care; he was just useless at putting those feelings into words. Yes. Feelings. Having stirred them into life, Rosy had left him with an entire legacy of feelings to catch up on, and others yet to face.

His PA called and Xander stabbed at his phone. 'Why didn't you tell me she'd left Switzerland?' he raged at Peter.

'I did tell you,' the ever-temperate Peter reminded him. 'Only after you'd already bought them tickets back to Praxos,' he ground out, almost losing control of the tsunami of unaccustomed feelings attacking him.

He apologised to Peter for his outburst, and was met by the merest murmur of Peter's calming voice. He valued the man too much to risk him leaving, and if anyone was responsible for this mess, it was Xander.

Romanos had told him once that friendship was like a plant that needed water, if you wanted it to thrive. *'How much more does that apply to love?'* Romanos had asked him. *'You can't expect a seed to grow and flourish if you stamp on it constantly. Plants need care all the time, not just when it suits you.'*

Growling, he threw his head back on the torturous sofa. Did he even deserve Rosy's friendship after everything he'd put her through? He was running the risk of losing the best thing that had ever happened to him, but might that be the best thing for Rosy? Could he salvage anything? Did he deserve her? Was he even capable of change? *Theós!* He had few enough likeable qualities.

Am I worthy of love?

Love? Inwardly, he did a double take. All the old doubts rushed in, to assure him that he was the least worthy of love of anyone he knew. Either that or he was a jinx, as he had suspected for some time.

Was this love?

Whatever it was, he'd never felt like this before—had never wanted to share experiences with anyone before. Nothing could come close to sharing Rosy's laughter, to feeling her warmth and compassion. No one else was so much fun, or half so sexy. Just seeing her eyes light up at something he'd said, or something she'd thought of and wanted to share, made him smile now.

And he realised he trusted her completely. When had he ever confided in anyone about anything? Eleni and Romanos, yes, but not to the extent that he'd shared with Rosy, exposing his fears and vulnerability as a child. No one could be allowed to see inside his head and know that the master of all he surveyed still had the ghost of a frightened child inside him. Yet it had seemed like the most natural thing in the world to confide in Rosy.

Unfolding his tense frame, he held up his phone in front of him to make a call. His hand hovered over the call button. Apparently, this titan of the business world was somewhat less sure-footed when it came to matters of the heart.

In the end, making the most important decision of his life turned out to be surprisingly easy.

She hadn't just settled in, she'd come home, Rosy reflected, smiling wistfully as she walked to school across the beach on the first morning of the new term. If only Xander were here, everything would be perfect. Happiness and a sense of belonging wasn't just down to the welcome she and her father had received, or even the watery winter sunshine and crystalline surf. Seeing her father happy and more settled than she could remember since her mother died only added to a deep-seated certainty that Praxos was where she belonged.

Early light sparkling on the surf carried the promise of a new day full of surprises. It lightened her heart to know that her father had already fallen in love with Praxos. When he'd discovered that many of the islanders he'd chatted to could do with some help with their gardens his future was rosy, he'd told Rosy with a wink and a grin.

But still a heavy sigh escaped her. She must learn to live without Xander.

Really?

Yes, *really*, she informed her inner voice with an accepting twist of her mouth. He hadn't made any attempt to contact her for the second time, and now she was done. It was over. She'd better learn to live without him—and fast.

The school morning began with Rosy taking a group of excited children for a walk to see what they could find on the beach. The outing was a great success and, with heads full of discoveries, they skipped back up the path to the school for lunch.

She had her hand on the famous gate when she heard it. There was only one person who arrived on Praxos by helicopter. Rosy's heart clenched. It was all very well telling herself she could handle this, but she'd made that same decision so many times as she'd repeatedly attempted to ignore what she now thought of as her doomed connection to a man who would never feel the same way about her. Xander's casual disregard for whatever it was they had enjoyed for that short, precious time was both hurtful and damaging, and she'd come back to Praxos to start again, turn the page, to give her father the best possible chance of a lasting recovery. Not to rekindle her affair with Xander.

And yet just knowing Xander was close by brought the world into sharper focus, as if everything had been infused with his energy and couldn't be avoided, any more than he could.

'Would you like me to take over for you?' Alexa offered.

'No...' Rosy forced a smile. 'I'm in no hurry to go anywhere except back to school.'

But Alexa refused to be so easily deterred. 'Don't you want to see him?' she asked bluntly.

They both knew who she was talking about.

'I'm sure Xander will make his presence felt soon enough.' Understatement. There would be rejoicing on the island tonight, as everyone loved Xander and would be pleased that he'd come back. He'd probably show up in the village square to share a drink with his neighbours. He was one of them. Here, and in Switzerland, was where he was most relaxed. He'd be impatient to slough off all the pretension of his billionaire lifestyle and to be with real people again—people he really cared about. It was just a pity that Xander didn't seem to care enough about himself.

Had she tried hard enough to heal him?

Have you tried hard enough to heal yourself?

I don't need healing, she informed her inner self firmly.

Rosy just needed her father to be happy, and for him to love Praxos as she did. Nothing was more important than seeing him embark on a miraculous new life. And the school was growing every day. Islanders who'd left Praxos, thanks to Achilles, had started to return from the mainland, and she wouldn't do anything to risk that.

Which meant maintaining a distance from Xander, Rosy reminded herself as the sound of rotor blades died away. He was still grieving the loss of Eleni and Romanos, which left him unable, or maybe not wanting, to love her back. For the sake of her own emotional health, she had to let go of the hope that they could ever enjoy a fulfilling relationship. Which was unfortunate. Unfortunate? A mild word to describe such a life-changing development, especially considering her circumstances.

She'd just completed her second pregnancy test and, like the first, it was positive. Her heart had leapt and sang when she first saw the result, but what would Xander say? Was he even capable of caring about a child—*his* child? She was already in love with the tiny mite growing safe inside her, but the urge to protect that child was strong, which meant she wouldn't rush into telling Xander. She'd choose her moment, and hope beyond hope he'd feel something.

Thinking about Xander brought a great wave of love washing over her. If only they could be a family, a real family. She'd always wondered if she'd even recognise love before he'd come along. Now she knew that loving without any expectation of having that love returned was love in its purest form.

And the baby? She could handle being a single mother. She had a good life here on Praxos, a life that wasn't dependent on Xander. With childcare, she could remain at the school, and her father would be a fantastic granddad. What more could she want?

Xander? Xander to be part of it all.

And what was the chance of that? Zero. There was no point in fretting and wanting more out of life when she already had so much to be thankful for.

CHAPTER SIXTEEN

SPOTTING ROSY IN the square hit him like a punch in the solar plexus. He'd been searching for her since he'd arrived, fielding greetings from his friends with one eye on the crowd.

His gut churned with relief that she was safe—relief that she'd come home—and, for once in his ordered, controlled life, uncertainty as to how she would greet him.

'Hey…' He walked right up to her, standing close enough to inhale her wildflower scent while leaving enough space for her to slip away without embarrassment should she want to.

She didn't leave.

'Hey yourself,' she murmured, cheeks pinking as she stared up into his face with the searing honesty he loved about her.

But there was more than that in her eyes. There was a change, an additional look of maturity he hadn't seen before, together with compassion and genuine concern for him that he certainly didn't deserve. He would never deserve Rosy. What was he even doing here? The decision he'd made to come back to see her had seemed an easy decision at the time, but now it seemed wrong, because he ran the risk of hurting her if he wasn't good enough for her.

'What happened to the new specs?' he asked, seeing the old damaged pair was back in place, along with the tightly wound hairdo, causing his heart to twinge.

She grimaced. 'Sorry, I broke them. I'll pay you back for them, of course.'

'No need,' he said, frowning as he wondered how a pair of thrift shop spectacles could evoke such powerful emotion in him. Rosy was like quicksilver, always interesting, always changing, but today he sensed something more. What wasn't she telling him? 'Are you hungry?'

'Always,' she admitted. 'You?'

'Always,' he echoed, glad she was at least willing to speak to him.

'Good.'

She sounded flat—or maybe wary. Who could blame her for feeling that way? He was hardly Mr Dependable outside of a business environment, was he?

'Shall we?' she invited, staring off towards a pop-up stall offering a selection of Greek delicacies.

'How's your father settling in?' he asked as they munched.

'Like a dream. He loves it here.' Her face was suddenly illuminated with simple happiness that made him feel good too. 'He's gardening up a storm at the school,' she explained, 'as well as working for a number of the islanders. It's like a miracle. I can't thank you enough.'

But…? he wondered as she paused and stared off into the middle distance.

'You don't have to thank me.'

'That's right, I don't. Because I'm staff,' she said.

'I hope you're teasing?' he said uncertainly.

She smiled a little sadly, he thought, but she didn't reply.

'I'm pleased he's settling in so well.' He studied her face, trying to read her guarded expression, and told himself to be glad that she'd returned to the island with her life back on track. 'Why do you wear these?' he asked, touching the side arm of her spectacles. 'Why not lenses?'

'Perhaps I like the distance they put between me and the rest of the world? Joke,' she added, but then she frowned. 'At least, I think I'm joking.'

Again, he got that feeling that she was keeping something important from him. Rosy had a rare combination of vulnerability and strength. So confident when it came to helping others, she sometimes doubted herself, and he hadn't exactly helped to eliminate that doubt with his behaviour.

They both stared off, as if seeking a distraction. The local band provided one by starting to play, which brought the islanders crowding onto the dance floor. The urge to have Rosy in his arms was one he couldn't fight—didn't want to fight.

'Dance?' he suggested with a casual shrug.

'I'd love to, but my dance card is full.'

Truth or lie? Either way, the result was not good. And then she was called away, apparently to discuss a vital matter regarding her father's plan to grow more seedlings in an unused shed.

'Sorry, Xander, can't be helped.'

Was he being given the run-around? When had any

woman ever done that? There was none of the usual humour and warmth in Rosy's eyes when she looked at him. She'd never had a problem with meeting his gaze before, but this was not the same Rosy he'd left in Gstaad. Had he blown it? Was it already too late to tell her how he felt about her? His heart sank into his handmade shoes.

He spent the rest of the night acting as if everything in his world was as it should be, while Rosy did her best to avoid him. All he wanted was Rosy. She occupied every part of his mind. His gaze followed her with a mix of bemusement, affront and naked longing. The only way to sort this out, he knew, was by risking his pride and making his feelings clear. Having anticipated a reunion that would rock both their worlds, he now faced a night on his own.

She called him the next day, and once again he got the feeling she was saying one thing when there were other, far more important things she'd like to say to him. So what was holding her back? She'd always been so upfront before. He had been relaxing back in the chair in Romanos's study, but now he was sitting bolt upright, paying keen attention.

'What can I do for you?'

'I thought it was time I made good on my outstanding auction lot. Cook you dinner?' she prompted as his mind raced.

Progress? Yeah. Definitely. After her distance last night, this was huge progress. But if they were finally getting together, he wanted the night to be perfect, and not have Rosy slogging away in the kitchen.

'Wouldn't you rather go out for a meal?'

'I'm not asking you out on a date.'

This time, he could read her tone perfectly, and it was practical Rosy all the way. She owed him dinner and was only offering to fulfil that pledge. It felt like a slap in the face.

'In view of your very generous donation, I have to hold up my end of the deal. I'm not promising cordon bleu, but I'm hoping it will be decent enough. I thought it would be nice to tie it in with celebrating my father's decision to make his home here on Praxos.'

And? What was she leaving out? He sensed there was more to the timing of the invitation than Rosy was prepared to let on. But, apart from the fact that he appeared to be an add-on to the celebration, she knew exactly what she was doing; by mentioning her father, she'd made it impossible for Xander to refuse.

'That's very kind of you,' he replied in the same formal tone she was using. 'I'm pleased to accept.'

'Good. Tonight. Eight o'clock prompt.'

There was a hint of urgency in her voice. He chose to ignore it in favour of wondering why on earth he'd made himself sound so formal. *Pleased to accept?* What was this, a royal appointment? It might as well have been. Turned out, he was not every woman's dream, and this woman could discard him as easily as he had walked away from others in the past.

Whatever her feelings for Xander—however many times he'd kicked her heart into touch—she knew she had to tell him about the baby. She would not withhold a truth like that from him for long. And she could never forget that he'd saved her father, which made it doubly right to have him at the dinner table tonight. It would be a test for her heart and what it longed for, but the group setting meant she'd be kept busy, making it easier to be around him, giving her a chance to compose herself before telling Xander afterwards, when they were alone, that she was pregnant with his child. She would also reassure him that she could do this by herself, and that as far as she was concerned their relationship was over. She had no intention of hanging on to the bitter end.

She kept the meal simple, knowing there was no chance she could impress a man for whom three Michelin star dining was commonplace. This was for her father too, and he preferred simple, tasty meals. The evening arrived all too fast, but she was ready—for whatever lay ahead.

Xander brought flowers. He'd picked them himself, according to Maria. Rosy put them in pride of place in the centre of the dining table and then stood back to admire them, while Alexa and Maria exchanged approving glances. Her dear friends were wasting their time. Xander was just being his usual charming self. He was charming to the guesthouse owners too, and to her father, saying what an honour it was to be included in the celebration, with no mention made of the huge sum of money he'd donated for the privilege.

Was everything working out the way she'd hoped? If she could just speak to him alone at some point, then maybe...

The kitchen had become her sanctuary, Rosy's small, private space, where she'd rehearsed what she was going to say to Xander, and where she could attempt to come to terms with how stunning he looked in dark jeans, and with his shirt sleeves rolled back to reveal the hard-muscled arms that had held her safe so many times...

She yelped as the distraction caused one of her pans to burn dry.

'Can I help you with that?'

Her entire body froze and burned at once, as Xander entered the kitchen.

'Here—oven glove,' she managed somehow to blurt out.

Brushing her hair back with her forearm as he settled the smoking pan safely on a trivet, she tried not to notice how close he was, or to register the familiar clean, warm man scent. Lifting her chin to thank him, she found his gaze fixed on her face.

'This isn't the time,' he began hesitantly, 'but I know when something's wrong. And I don't mean a burnt pan—'

'There's nothing wrong!' Except for the fact that all those rehearsed words had suddenly deserted her. Putting some much-needed space between them, she reached for another pan.

'Rosy, please—don't do this.'

'Don't do what?' she asked, firming her jaw.

'Don't act as if nothing's wrong. I can't bear this distance between us. I admit it's my fault. I've never been good at expressing my feelings, while you give so generously, without ever expecting anything back.'

The small flame of hope that had somehow survived, and had even revived with the news they were expecting a child together, flickered and died, because she did want something back. She longed for something from

Xander. Just because she didn't demand anything surely didn't mean she deserved nothing.

'Be with me,' he exclaimed suddenly, taking hold of her arms to stare intently into her eyes. 'I want to wake up with you next to me every morning for the rest of my life—'

'Next to a man who can't tell me that he loves me, because of some childhood trauma in his past? I'm sorry, Xander. I can't do that.'

'I'll give you the earth—'

This impassioned declaration made Rosy sadder than ever. What was it with love? Was love taboo for all time, for Xander? One thing was certain, this was not the time to tell him about the baby. Instead, she turned to the practical.

'Could you carry these plates in for me, please?'

'Plates?' Xander stared at her as if she were talking an alien language until, with a shake of his head, he walked away.

Rosy had gone to so much trouble to make the meal a success and everyone was enjoying it, but Xander didn't taste a thing. Maria kept giving him sideways glances, as did Alexa. It was hard to maintain a polite front when his brain was scrambled. Throughout his life he'd had plenty of knock-backs, and had vowed to have no more, but Rosy, remaining true to her principles, had refused to be impressed by anything he'd said. *Theós!* He'd laid his heart on the line, but she'd turned him down, and even though she'd remained scrupulously polite to him throughout the meal, Rosy gave him no hope of anything more.

Even so, he invited her to take a walk when the meal ended and everything was cleared away. Several pairs of sympathetic eyes swivelled his way when Rosy shook her head, saying, 'I have to make coffee—'

'I can do that,' Maria interrupted.

And she did, but Rosy went to help her, leaving him hanging, making polite conversation, though he barely knew what he was saying until she returned.

'Xander?' Rosy prompted. 'Coffee?'

'Please,' he said grimly.

'It's to be hoped the dancing cheers you up,' Alexa commented.

He let that pass. A couple of local musicians had turned up to join the party, and he gathered there'd be dancing in the yard shortly. Dancing was the very last thing he was in the mood for. Since Rosy had rejected him, he couldn't think about anything else. How could he make this right? Could he express himself in a way she would believe?

'Something's upset you,' he said when everyone else had left the table to dance.

'Has it?'

'Rosy... Don't we know each other better than that?' She shook her head.

'Can we take a walk? Chat? Please?'

'About what, Xander?'

'You and me?'

'There is no you and me. We are two separate individuals living very different lives.'

'It doesn't have to be like that.'

'We've been through this,' she reminded him. 'I want

more than you can give. I would like to talk to you—but not here.'

'The beach?' he suggested.

'Fine.'

If he didn't change he stood to lose everything—Rosy and his plans for the future, to improve the school on Praxos, as well as others across the world, and all thanks to his obsessive focus on building his business empire. Yet his various business interests could function perfectly well without him, thanks to the excellent teams he'd put in place. So why couldn't he build a successful personal relationship? Was he so damaged that he always had to identify a goal—in this case Rosy—and treat her as if she were just another business deal to secure? Was he incapable of appreciating this woman as a unique and precious human being? *Theós!* She wasn't a spreadsheet detailing profit and loss.

He stood watching and admiring as she gave one last fond glance around her guests. Her father was dancing with Alexa, which made him smile too. Everyone was having the best time, but Rosy still had shadows in her eyes, he noticed when she turned back to him. Had he put them there?

'Shall we go?' she suggested. 'I don't think we'll be missed, do you?'

He was too busy wondering about the shadows in Rosy's eyes. Was he fated to carry the past with him for ever, at the risk of hurting more innocent souls like Rosy?

'Come on,' she urged, tension ringing in her voice.

Perhaps they could get to the bottom of what was troubling her when they had some privacy on the shore.

If he lost this opportunity, he doubted it would come around again. Rosy was a free spirit who did as she liked. Right now, she was hurrying ahead of him, head down, back tense, as if she had the weight of the world on her shoulders.

It was a relief to see her kick off her sandals to cool her heels in the surf.

CHAPTER SEVENTEEN

THE SEA HAD always had the power to soothe her before, but with so many words and thoughts swirling in her head, and Xander standing close to her but not touching, where she could feel his tension, knowing she was the cause, left her feeling worse than ever.

If she'd been frank with him from the start and admitted she was falling in love with him, how much easier would it have been to tell him about their baby?

What would he say if she did that? *It's too soon for me—this was never part of the plan.*

Maybe his return to Praxos was an experiment that had failed. If that were the case, she'd get over it—she'd have to, for her baby's sake, for her father, and for the school.

And for you, Rosy's annoying inner voice insisted. *It's time you thought about yourself for a change. If you don't, you won't be ready to care for a child.*

'Fate has a dark sense of humour,' she remarked as she stared out to sea.

'Meaning?' Xander enquired.

'Throwing us together.' And igniting a passion so bright and strong she doubted anyone could have resisted it, but a passion that strong could blow itself out just as quickly as it had begun, and the last thing she wanted for their child was uncertainty.

'Perhaps fate has more sense than we do.'

She hummed with doubt, and her sigh was the sigh of a realist who had accepted that their lives were on very different tracks that could never meet.

'If you don't stop biting your lip you're going to make it sore,' Xander observed. 'Are you going to tell me what's wrong, or are you going to keep it to yourself all night? I might be able to help you, but I can't do anything unless I understand, and for that you have to trust me with whatever it is you've got on your mind—'

'I'm pregnant.'

It seemed for ever until he spoke, and then he said softly, 'Are you sure?'

'Positive. Condoms can fail. They obviously did. I've taken two tests,' she explained.

'How do you feel about it?' he asked carefully.

How did *he* feel about it?

'It's life-changing news—but wonderful,' she said honestly. 'I don't think I've ever been so happy in my life. I wanted you to know right away, but things...' Her voice tailed off as she tried to read him.

'Things got in the way,' he supplied. 'Because I went away.'

'Yes.'

Xander was frowning deeply, as if all his doubts and fears had landed in one great blow. 'Do you need anything?'

If he offered money, she might crumble and never recover.

'Anything at all, Rosy?'

Yes. Obviously. I need you!

Hit by a surge of emotion, Rosy was astonished by the strength of the mother love flooding her mind. Their child was more than an accident or a trick of mischievous fate, it was a precious individual, and one she already loved. Did Xander feel nothing at all for their baby?

'I don't need anything,' she said calmly. *Except your love.* 'I hope you will acknowledge your child, but other than that—'

'You don't want anything for yourself—you never have!' Xander exclaimed. 'But you should—*you should*!'

With that, he grabbed her close—so close she couldn't breathe, so close it was he who stepped back, aghast that he might have hurt her.

'Forgive me,' he begged, drawing her to him again, this time with such care and gentleness he made her feel as if she were the most precious thing on earth to him. Exhaling with frustration, he admitted, 'All these years I've closed myself off from feeling any emotion, defending myself against ghosts from the past. In continuing to do that, I almost lost you. Can we start again? For the sake of our child, and for your sake most of all, because you deserve everything I can give you and more, will you give me the chance to prove to you that I can change, and that I do love you, Rosy—so much, in fact, that it frightens me. Me,' he exclaimed with bemusement and a shake of his head. 'What an idiot I've been, never once telling you how much I love you.' Cupping her face in his big, rough hands, Xander stared steadily into her eyes. 'I love you, Rosy. I love you with all my heart. Can you ever forgive me for taking so long to put feelings I'd thought lost for ever into words?'

Rosy's compassion soared. 'Of course. That's what love is.' She only had to think back to Xander's childhood, when it had been a battle to stay alive. 'With the life you've had, it's no wonder you buried yourself in business, and ruthlessly erased anything to do with emotion.'

'Enough about me. I only want to talk about you.' Taking both her hands in his, Xander spoke quietly, intently. 'I've missed you, Rosy. It's as simple, and as complicated as that. Our separation taught me I never want to be apart again. But—' He hesitated and stared out to sea before admitting, 'When it comes to the baby, I'll need your help. I'm a novice, with no idea how to raise a child.'

'We'll learn together,' she said, but it was tragic to see the man she loved broken by thoughts of inadequacy when it came to his unborn child. Xander needed to know that their baby would never be as vulnerable as he had once been. 'Babies don't come with a How-To manual,' she teased gently, feeling relief when she saw the flicker of a smile touch his lips. 'Ours is a child created by love, that will be loved by both of us equally. We'll learn together,' she promised.

Xander's expression changed again. 'Why would you do that? Why would you forgive me for all the hurt I've caused you?'

'Because that's what you do for someone you love.'

'You love me too?'

'Of course I love you. Can't you tell?'

Xander dropped to his knees on the sand. 'Then will you make me the happiest man on earth?'

Rosy knelt down took and took hold of Xander's hands. Searching the eyes of the man she loved, this master of all he surveyed, quite literally brought to his knees by love, she knew without hesitation that this was right.

'Will you marry me?'

Xander's question was straightforward, but the expression in his eyes was not. There was still the faintest trace of fear that she might say no, as if the boy Romanos had rescued all those years ago had not been completely saved, but had been acting out a role in order to secure his foothold in Romanos's world. By the time Xander had felt his position in that life was safe, the act had become his norm. It might take a lifetime to reassure him, but a lifetime was what she would give.

'I love you, and of course my answer's yes.'

Xander's black gaze had never been more compelling, the connection between them more complete. Whatever they had faced in the past dwindled in the expectation of a new life together.

'A fresh start,' he murmured.

'And for the first time we're on an equal footing,' she pointed out, wondering if it was possible for a heart to actually burst with happiness.

'Explain,' Xander said as he stared deep into her eyes in a way that made her want to kiss him, rather than talk.

'Neither of us has a clue what to do where babies are concerned, so we'll learn together. We're not much good at expressing our feelings, but we'll learn to get better at that too.' And then she couldn't resist teasing him again, if only to see the smile return to his stern mouth. 'It will all be fine, if you do the heavy lifting and I'm the brains of the operation—'

She should have known he'd tumble her onto the sand beneath him.

'How are we going to explain this?' she said as he kissed her over and over again.

'The sand on our clothes? I'll say you were cheeky, and I had to punish you by putting you over my knee—'

'And risk the combined wrath of the island seniors?'

Xander's lips quirked wickedly as he shrugged. 'I'm not worried. I'll have you to protect me.'

She laughed as he kissed her again.

'Just to get this straight,' she said, pulling away briefly. 'Will you ever punish me?'

'In so many ways,' Xander promised in a sexy drawl.

'We'd better get back,' she said with a deep blush, linking their fingers.

'Yes, and don't forget, you have a wedding to arrange, followed by a trip to New York.'

'New York?' she exclaimed.

'To begin with, yes, and then maybe we'll visit my private Caribbean island.'

'Only maybe?' she teased, before remembering that quite possibly Xander did own his own Caribbean island. Some people had property portfolios, while Xander Tsakis collected more than she could even imagine. They could put a Caribbean island to good use, Rosy realised, her mind already racing on ahead to encompass holidays for disadvantaged children just like Xander had been.

'I know what you're thinking,' he said.

'Oh?' Her mind had already moved on to much, *much* later, when the dinner party had ended, everyone had gone home and they were finally alone.

'You can take the girl out of the teacher, but you can never take the teacher out of the girl,' Xander revealed knowingly as he drew her close again.

'Or the good man finding happiness at last. For ever,' she whispered as Xander dipped his head to kiss her.

'And always,' he pledged.

EPILOGUE

THERE WERE NO words to describe how wonderful their wedding on the island had been, Rosy reflected as Xander's jet soared into the sky. She'd worn a simple cream ankle-length sliver of silk, hand-sewn by Alexa, which both Astrid and Maria had embellished with tiny seed pearls around the modest neckline. The children at the school had supplied her bouquet, picking wildflowers they'd secured with flowing pastel-coloured ribbons. Rosy's father had given her away with all the pride of a man who had found himself at last, and who actually liked the man he had become.

With her feet bare and fresh flowers in her hair—and, yes, wearing lenses for once, rather than her tatty old specs, to fully take in the beauty of the scene, including the stunning good looks of the most handsome man on the face of the earth, waiting for her beneath an arch of flowers, Rosy could only thank fate, as well as Xander's adoptive parents, for bringing them together, and for allowing him to become the man she was so happy to marry.

Xander had dressed for the occasion in an ivory linen suit with a single white rose in his buttonhole. Only the islanders had watched on, with Rosy's father, who was one of them now. A fleet of local fishermen had kept the paparazzi at bay, and everyone declared it to be the most beautiful wedding they had ever attended.

And now she was embarking on a new adventure with the man she loved, and their beloved child growing safe inside her.

'Happy?' Xander asked as their aircraft soared above the clouds.

'So happy, I can't even put it into words,' Rosy admitted.

There were no words to describe how she felt, any more than there was a recipe for love, other than to say that their love was a deep and abiding certainty between two people who would always put each other before themselves. When Xander leaned over to kiss her she was the happiest woman on earth, because they were both free at last; they'd freed each other and would never hide their feelings again.

There was nothing low-key about this trip to New York. They were travelling in the largest of Xander's fleet of private jets. Complete with two bedrooms and two bathrooms, it had a comfortable seating area and a dining table, where they were waited on by a cordon bleu chef.

'Sparkling water for two,' Xander murmured as they shared a knowing and loving look above a pair of fine crystal flutes.

For ever and always. That was their toast. And as Rosy stared at the simple platinum bands they both wore, she knew that the ghosts of the past couldn't touch them.

* * *

The biggest surprise was yet to come. After their first exhilarating morning in New York, Xander took Rosy to see one of the schools he was supporting, which had a strikingly similar ethos to their school on Praxos. Every day of his life, whether he knew it or not, Xander was a living tribute to Romanos. From there, after promising the children that they would return and hoped to see them in Praxos for an exchange trip very soon, they went to view an apartment overlooking Central Park.

'Do you like it?' Xander asked.

'How could I not? It's fabulous,' Rosy breathed as she took in the view over the park. 'What's this?' she exclaimed as Xander dropped a key into her hand.

'Whenever you need space, or when you're supervising a school exchange programme, this serviced apartment is yours to use as you please.'

'Mine?' She laughed disbelievingly. 'No. It's too much.'

'It's not nearly enough for the woman who saved me from myself,' Xander argued, furrowing his brow.

'If you're not careful, I might start believing you,' she teased as she stroked a loving hand down his cheek.

'Believe me,' Xander assured her. 'You've no idea what you have done for me.' Placing his strong hand over her still flat belly, he explained. 'A family always felt like a dream too far for me.'

'You had dreams?' She shook her head sadly to think of the child he had once been, alone and longing for a family to call his own.

Xander shrugged. 'Like everyone else has dreams? Of course.'

To think of him daydreaming took some doing, but she was beginning to understand the workings of Xander's psyche, and guessed that even before they'd met he must have allowed himself time off from those spreadsheets to plan all the good things he'd done for so many people over the years.

'My first dream was to climb out of the gutter,' he revealed without prompting. 'My next was to repay the man who helped me to do that.'

'Romanos,' Rosy guessed. 'He did so much for both of us.'

'And lately I had another dream, that began to seem like an impossible goal.'

'Tell me—'

'To marry you,' he said as he brought her into his arms.

They returned from their honeymoon to a surprise celebration on Praxos. Everyone had accepted that Xander and Rosy had wanted a simple wedding, but now it was the islanders' turn to show their love for the bridal pair. A new time of plenty had arrived, thanks to Xander, who was only too eager to share his good fortune with the people he loved.

Eighteen months later, Xander threw another huge party to celebrate the first birthday of their first child, a beautiful little flame-haired girl called Stella.

That heady night produced gorgeously wild twin sons, Darius and Jago. So now they were five, and Xander marked the occasion of their fifth wedding anniversary by giving Rosy a stunning emerald ring, surrounded by flashing blue-white diamonds.

He had chosen the central stone to match the colour of Rosy's eyes, he explained.

'So you are a romantic after all. I knew it!' she declared in triumph.

As well, he was the most amazing father. Watching him playing with their children on the lush green lawn at the Big House, while she relaxed because she was expecting another baby, Rosy couldn't have been happier, for him, for them. No surprise that she was pregnant again. How was she supposed to resist this man? How could she resist having another gorgeous child with him?

Occasionally, the irony of their situation made them laugh. 'Perhaps you should go away from time to time,' she had jokingly suggested to Xander on more than one occasion when he took her to bed. But that was never going to happen because, true to his word, if Xander went away, he arranged cover for Rosy at the school and their children came with them. There was a new teacher at the school, a vivacious young woman called Anna-Maria, who had grown close to Xander's PA, Peter. Rosy's father had found companionship too, and was often found out and about with Alexa.

Things couldn't have worked out any better, Rosy reflected. She was still working part-time at the school, which Stella now attended, with the twins just enrolled in the nursery class, and she intended to carry on working. There wasn't just one school exchange to arrange now, but several across the world, with yet more planned. Marriage hadn't put a curb on Rosy's zeal for teaching; in fact, Xander's passion for educating children matched her own.

But it was this man who made her heart sing, she reflected, smiling happily as Xander approached, giving a piggyback ride to Stella, with the twins in his arms. The child growing beneath her protective hands, along with their three blessings, Stella, Darius and Jago, currently scrambling over their father and screaming like mad, meant she wouldn't change a thing.

Having extricated himself from the rumble, Xander came up to her with a wriggling twin under each arm, and Stella still straddling his shoulders. This man was her soulmate, her most trusted confidante, the love of her life as well as the person she had the most fun with.

How they'd changed, she reflected as they all ended up in a laughing heap on the velvety grass. From wary and mistrustful, to each being one half of a wonderful whole—one life, one heart that could never be divided. Staring at Xander with love in her eyes, she thought that in the time they'd been together his rugged good looks had only improved, from heart-stoppingly hot to bone-meltingly incredible. She told him so.

'How would you know?' Xander teased as he carefully lowered their children to the ground. 'You've lost your specs again.'

'I don't need twenty-twenty vision to know a very hot, very bad man when I see one.'

'If you weren't already pregnant, I'd call the nanny to take the children, so I could make you pregnant again.'

'We could try for twins,' she teased.

'That's it, I'm calling for their nanny,' Xander warned.

Embracing their lively children, she laughed into his eyes. 'They're begging for an ice cream, so I really think you should.'

* * * * *

If you couldn't get enough of
Untouched Until the Greek's Return
*then you'll love these other stories
by Susan Stephens!*

Kidnapped for the Acosta Heir
Forbidden to Her Spanish Boss
The Playboy Prince of Scandal
One Scandalous Christmas Eve
A Bride Fit for a Prince?

Available now!

#4185 THE SECRET OF THEIR BILLION-DOLLAR BABY
Bound by a Surrogate Baby
by Dani Collins

Sasha married billionaire Rafael Zamos to escape her stepfather's control. But is the gilded cage of her convenient union any better? Lost within their marital facade, Sasha fiercely protects her heart while surrendering to her husband's intoxicating touch... Might a child bring them closer?

#4186 THE KING'S HIDDEN HEIR
by Sharon Kendrick

Emerald Baker was a cloakroom attendant when she spent one mind-blowing night with a prince. Now Konstandin is a king—and he insists that Emmy marry him when she tells him he is a father! For the sake of her son, she'll consider his ruthlessly convenient proposal...

#4187 A TYCOON TOO WILD TO WED
The Teras Wedding Challenge
by Caitlin Crews

All innocent Brita Martis craves is freedom from her grasping family, and marrying powerful Asterion Teras may be her best chance of escape. The chemistry that burns between them at first sight thrills her, but when their passion explodes, she is lost! Unless she can tame the wildest tycoon of all...

#4188 TWIN CONSEQUENCES OF THAT NIGHT
by Pippa Roscoe

When billionaire Nate Harcourt jets to Spain on business, he runs straight into his electrifying one-night stand from two years ago. Except Gabi Casas now has twins—his heirs! His childhood as an orphan taught Nate to trust nobody, but he wants better for his sons... so he drops to one knee!

#4189 CONTRACTED AND CLAIMED BY THE BOSS
Brooding Billionaire Brothers
by Clare Connelly

Former child star Paige Cooper now shuns fame and works as a nanny. When Australian pearl magnate and single father Max Stone hires her to help his daughter, she's shocked by her red-hot response to him. And as the days count down on Paige's contract, resistance is futile...

#4190 SAYING "I DO" TO THE WRONG GREEK
The Powerful Skalas Twins
by Tara Pammi

Ani's wedding will unlock her trust fund and grant her freedom—she just doesn't expect infuriatingly attractive Xander at the altar! Penniless, Ani can't afford to walk away. Their craving for each other might be as hot as her temper, but can she risk falling for a man who scorns love?

#4191 A DIAMOND FOR HIS DEFIANT CINDERELLA
by Lorraine Hall

Matilda Willoughby's guardian, ultra-rich Javier Alatorre, is determined to marry her off before her twenty-fifth birthday. Otherwise he must marry her himself! As she clashes with him at every turn, her burning hatred soon becomes scorching need. And Matilda is unprepared for how thin the line between love and hate really is!

#4192 UNDONE IN THE BILLIONAIRE'S CASTLE
Behind the Billionaire's Doors...
by Louise Fuller

Ivo Faulkner has a business deal to close. Except after his explosive night with Joan Santos, his infamous laser focus is nowhere to be found! He invites her to his opulent castle to exorcise their attraction, but by indulging their temptation, Ivo risks being unable to ever let his oh-so-tempting Cinderella go...

YOU CAN FIND MORE INFORMATION ON UPCOMING HARLEQUIN TITLES, FREE EXCERPTS AND MORE AT HARLEQUIN.COM.

HPCNMRB0224